Jane Skelton grew up in Queensland in a series of country towns. She has published short fiction in various literary journals and anthologies over the past 20 years. Her novel *earth eaters* was a winner of the 2010 Varuna LitLink Unpublished Manuscript Award. She is currently completing another novel. Jane was a recipient of a Literature Board (Australia Council) grant which assisted her in completing *earth eaters*, and was awarded an Australia Council 'ArtStart' award in 2012. She has a doctorate in Creative Arts (University of Western Sydney). She lives in the Blue Mountains, NSW with her partner and beloved dogs, and works in Western Sydney in the community sector.

PRAISE FOR JANE SKELTON

'Jane Skelton's *earth eaters* is an outstanding piece of writing. A naturalistic portrayal of country life in a tough environment, an isolated country area, combined with elements of the Gothic, playing with the earthiness of farm life – cows vulvas, bull's balls, dog shit – and the supernatural – ghosts of the earth eaters. Sex, birth, death, sickness violence, sexual molestation, eccentricity, strangeness, all handled with clarity and compassion ... the language and description have the precision of poetry – concrete, visceral, one could say earthy. The Gothic is set against a laconic Australian country understatement.'

—BARBARA BROOKS, writer & academic

'Jane Skelton's command of tone and language is excellent. The effect of striking metaphors and vivid metaphors in the midst of the generally quite flat, straightforward prose is like the effect of the dead, dry landscape which is nevertheless alive with its own meanings; and the house which is animate with its secret history.'

—DELYS BIRD, academic, editor, *Westerly*

'An intelligent, engagingly written and thought-provoking work ... absorbing.'

—DR BRONWEN LEVY, University of Qld, on Jane Skelton's novel manuscript, *1983*.

' ... a talent to watch.'

—WALTER MASON,
The Universal Heart Book Club

Spineless Wonders

BN01164417

PO Box 220 STRAWBERRY HILLS

New South Wales, Australia, 2012

www.shortaustralianstories.com.au

First published by Spineless Wonders 2013

Typeset in Adobe Garamond Pro

Printed and bound by Lightning Source Australia

\National Library of Australia Cataloguing-in-Publication entry

Lives of the Dead/Jane Skelton

1st ed.

978-0-9872546-8-9 (pbk.)

A823.4

JANE SKELTON

LIVES OF THE DEAD

spineless wonders
www.shortaustralianstories.com.au

to

Virginia Shepherd

with love

for living with these stories

... and the sea
Blinding me with its lights, the lives of the dead
Unreeling in it, spreading like oil.

Sylvia Plath
The Rabbit Catcher

CONTENTS

LIVES OF THE DEAD

The smell of regret hangs about the town. It drifts in on the hot wind out of the west and lingers, collects in corners, in the sheen on the hot road, in the wide open streets. At midday, there is the sound of cicadas, or sprinklers. Cars glint up the highway. Strings of jewels.

The smell gets stronger further in. Sparse and harsh-lit town. I cruise the streets, my tyres smooth on melting bitumen. The houses look astonished—they bulge with what is within. They have inhaled; are holding their breath. Sometimes a front door is open. The interiors are dark, a linoleum passage leads straight out to an open back door.

I am looking for my mother. My ute curves and slides round the town's map.

The old part of town feels familiar. Behind weathered shops, backyards drift into a disarray of paddocks stitched with limp barbed wire. I can taste the dryness. A lone horse lifts its head as I shoot past.

The Paradise Café is a dark cavern, the booths a warm silky-oak. The walls, papered with poster ads from the fifties, depict elegant women, their cigarettes poised between delicate fingers, held up to clean, smiling mouths. The old man is still alive, I see. He approaches with the tray, the teapot rugged in a fluffy wool cosy. Rattles a cup and saucer toward me. He hasn't recognised me.

'Do you know her?' I hold up the photo in its silver frame. The old man stares. His eyes shift from the photo to my face. His bleak, empty eyes. We regard each other. As his face begins to crumple, he turns, shuffles away. He is very old now, it is almost too late. Below his shorts his legs are shot with the oyster bulges of knotted veins.

I watch the old man retreat to the back of the cafe where bits of other rooms are glimpsed through an open door. Fear flickers, everything seems slowed down. A fly tastes its way across the sticky surface of my table. From the cafe's back rooms comes faint tv. laughter and quivering light. I sip my grey, metallic-tasting tea. I wonder what the hell I'm doing.

I see myself in the art deco mirror above the booth. My long hair is frizzed up on one side from the wind blasting through the open window of my ute. I'm exhausted, I've been driving for days.

I find a nondescript motel and crash. Spread-eagled on the double bed I see the highway's white line unreeling under my eyelids. Other highways superimpose upon the image like a travel scene in a fifties film. I'd followed the map-veins with my fingers: the bold dominating arteries; the delicate traceries of lesser roads. The creeks, rivers, tracks, bores, dams. The shadows of the Great Divide.

I took gravel roads over flat plains of shiny yellow grass; drove through towns with names like Dingo, Comet,

Emerald, Alpha, Cosmos, Prairie, Texas, Ohio. The towns were all the same. Flat, wide and staring at the sun. I was in them and out again. I drove well, hard and fast.

I drove along the coast, sashayed round headlands where the sea swept away from me, the waves spit-flecked, the beaches strewn with sea-weed and feathers.

I'd had trouble finding a way into the town. Things had changed, it was by-passed now. The highway veered close, then curved away, leaving the town alone in its valley. I could not turn around as it was a divided road, and drove for kilometres, through hard gravel hills, past dead trees that poked the sky. Every now and then I'd pass tiny wooden crosses, memorials placed by the families on the spots where their loved ones had died.

In the motel, all-night traffic hums in my head and car headlights slide across the curtained window. Footsteps rattle up and down stairs and patter across landings. I keep falling asleep then jerking awake; my feet kicking out at nothing.

Then I am hauling myself down on a rope of sunlight; through lolly green, over coral ridges, past fishes eating, scraping with numb mouths, over deep blue starfish soft as plush toys, over the velvet openings of clams. Caught by the current and driven onward, sucked through crevices, into a green mysterious valley—where I am suspended like a stupid fish, at rest at last, mouthing and blinking in warm delicious water.

I don't remember the rest of it—something wakes me—someone yelling in the night. Maybe it was me.

It is hot and bright at eight am. I stride the streets. Locals cluster at the traffic lights, and then disperse. Their shirts and dresses flash in the sun. Their faces are soft and without expression. I don't recognise anyone.

I look around for signs of my mother. Wander the supermarkets, the carparks, scan the glittering disarray of strewn trolleys. I search for signs of her in the empty shopping mall, where country and western muzak mumbles out of overhead speakers. It is different now, more modern, but here she once perused the shelves, her hands picked up cans, she read the labels, she opened up the cartons of eggs to make sure none were broken, chose oranges, squeezing gently to test their juiciness.

I walk past houses-Queensland style on stumps. Front yards are flat and bald. Sometimes, a dying palm-tree flaps out front, or a plaster Aborigine stands alone on a shaved lawn.

I visit her old house-a white weatherboard on stilts, its paint peeling like scabby skin, a concertina of part-open louvres down the side. She bought it after I left home, I've never lived here. She'd sent me a photo of herself, standing at the front door holding a cat. She was posing, one foot pointing out. The house was newly painted then, the yellow door framed her, a picture inside a picture. When I used to visit I'd sleep on the closed-in verandah, look out over the banana and custard apple trees, the oleanders. Ten years since I was last here. The trees are gone, the place looks drier, balder, like most of the yards here. I wonder who lives here now.

I'm being watched, a stranger, loitering in front of a house. I turn and look across the street, shading my eyes. Vertical blinds twitch across a window. Someone has pulled a string. Someone. I feel eyes on me. Eyes squint through cracks, through the mesh of fly screen. A cicada rhythm rattles on, escalates and dies.

By noon the streets are empty. I find the library. It is shut. I sit on the kerb under an enormous Moreton Bay fig. Two women walk toward me, across the wide street. One of them pushes a stroller and a toddler trots beside them. I watch them coming toward me, through the haze bubbling above the bitumen. It reduces them to stick figures. They never reach me.

Back in the motel I take the photo out of my bag. It is covered in a film of fine dust, and its corners are ratty and peeling. It is not properly framed but rather propped inside the silver frame.

There is a scratch, on the photo, across my mother's face and down her dress. I don't know if this mark was deliberate, it looks like someone rent her image with a pen, and the damage was later repaired. Perhaps a child had scribbled on it, maybe it was me. My parents, in the photo, are in waltz pose, both turned to face the camera. My father is wearing a pin-striped suit and hard-knotted tie, and has a tiny moustache. He clasps my mother's hand and covers it with his own. His other hand peeps at her back. He stands tall and firm. My mother's face stares over his chest; her breast is against his stomach. A thin black belt around her slim waist. The froth of her bright hair is the antithesis of my father's dark helmet. They both wear small, secretive smiles; their eyes are dreamy, hooded.

This is a photo of my parents at their happiest, their bright moon faces shine out of darkness. In the background are the unfocussed shapes of other dancers: a single leg descends from a dark dress, polished boards gleam, blurred islands of smashed light waver above my parents' heads.

It is an elegant black and white world out of an old movie. I don't know the photo's date. I guess it was during the

Second World War, or just after. I like to think of them on a ship, arrested in a world of waltzes and cocktails, where people are happy and slightly drunk, where it is always night, and old-time jazz drifts out above the gentle waves of a dark and endless sea.

In this town, the dead are more alive than the living.

In the Paradise Cafe, the old man is wearing an apron over his shorts, a long white apron streaked with yellow stains. Kids in school uniform troop in and buy lollies. One of them, two of 'em, one of 'em. Teeth, bananas, cobbers, musk-sticks, bullets raspberries, chickas. Sticky fingers stab the glass counter. The old man glances over at me, his face grey and sweaty as he ladles lollies into white paper bags. When he shuffles over with my milkshake, I ask again if he's seen my mother. He gapes at me, nods toward the back of the shop. I don't know if I want to go back there. I toy with my straw, stabbing the ice-cream and malt blobs, imagine that she's here, living in limbo at the back of the café.

What if she's like him, the old man. Changed into an automaton, or an undesirable aspect of herself. I tell myself it's a matter of perception. She will be what I want her to be. She will be the lady on the ship. Though then she might dislike me, my dishevelled hair, my untidiness. The old man and the children are turned toward me, staring, waiting.

I grew up in shops. I know the layout pretty well. There is a life going on out-back, in those rooms you can barely glimpse. My shopkeeper parents, in their middle years, lived in a series of country towns; smelt regret on the wind through fly screen. The sea was a long way off.

As a child I stood behind the hordes, pressed up to the counter, waiting. I skipped out-back, past the legs of my parents, the winking clock-hand creases in their pants, as they slid and swayed between deep-fry and laminex, shaking the fat off the chips. On humid, fluorescent-lit nights I stood in a blizzard of insects while Dad mopped the grease from the lino.

I ease out of my booth and stroll behind the counter, brush past the old man and through a door hung with tangled plastic strips. I enter a small, fuggy, cluttered room dominated by an old- fashioned tele, its veneer coating buckled, its big greenish screen reflecting the blob of my body. From the shop, an old fridge shudders and abruptly stops whining. A blowie pings against a window pane.

The old man hasn't followed me in, so I take a chance and frisk the joint. It is a room where every surface over many years has built up its layers of objects, put down at random and never taken up again. Everything salted with a fine dust blown in from across the country.

I scoop up a framed photo from amongst the china ornaments, empty pill bottles, used cotton buds and other crud on the dresser. It's a shot of the old man as a young bloke: a sepia, soft-jowled fellow in khaki. Lying beside it is a faded unframed, curling-up black and white snap. I dust it off.

In the photo a Holden station-wagon is parked on the edge of a gravel road. Leaning on the car a blond woman in a dark floral dress and white sandals has thrown back her head in laughter. Stuck above her left breast, a white flower. Propped against her, is a giggling young girl with a camera. The girl's shoulder presses into the woman's waist. The Holden's bonnet shimmers white. The car's shadow laps the white road. Behind them hills of soft brushed grass, low bushes and shivery stones rise to a line of washed-out telegraph poles.

In the photo, my mother and I and the photographer share a joke. Our faces are blurred, features indistinct. Our postures animated, excited. I am fingering the black strap of the Instamatic, hung around my neck. What does my camera's round eye see?

I hunt for clues in the photograph. The car's sheen is a mirror, reflecting a line of headland, a strip of sea and the shadows of people standing before us. Memories jolt me-the sweat patches on my mother's back, the upholstery, her dry hair in the wind's mouth, and us running, kicking up the sand, between the dunes and the sea.

Plastic strips clack as the old man enters. His eyes have retreated into shadows, his inward-turning lips tremble. He holds out his fist as he approaches, taking shuffle-steps. He unfolds his clenched fingers and in his palm, under my nose, is a matchbox. I take it, slide it open, and inside is a tiny sailing ship with masts of split matchsticks against a painted background of blue sky, clouds and gulls. The old man grunts, 'It was hers.' I turn from his gash of mouth, his furniture, his broken ornaments whose cold china eyes witnessed everything. He was my mother's boss after my father died. I'd always suspected that she was having an affair with him.

I want to grab the old man's bony shoulders and shake him. He stands, his face is bewildered. He's just the round-shouldered old bloke who runs the cafe.

I shove past him and run through his house, in and out of rooms, feet thumping on lino. But the old man's rooms are empty, his pressed-tin ceilings hold nothing down.

I stand in a windowless room in the middle of the house, in the semi-darkness. It is somehow safe, here in the half-light, in the dusk-like stillness. The mumble of music comes from somewhere far away; a slow rhythm, slower than a heartbeat. The salt-blood pulses in the veins of the dancers.

The couples revolve, under the moon-sail, moving through islands of light, islands of darkness.

I close the door on their low and secret laughter. Out in the passage is a smell of damp face-powder.

I find the back door and reel outside. Under a brazen sky, iron roofs dazzle. The old man's waiting for me. He's in his black jacket, the one he wore at the funeral, too loose on him now, and stinking of mould. I follow him up the yard, through the fence and across the paddock, under the staccato laughter of crows. Out to the highway, to her cross. Her cross. Still shored up by bunches of faded plastic flowers and stained jars that once held holy water.

'You did this to her, Murderer.' I hiss it out at him. I've wanted to say this for a long time. After all, he had been the one driving.

The old man backs away, hobbles off down the paddock until I can no longer tell him from the crows. I kneel until the gravel pierces my knees. I take up a fistful and shower it over my head. That squirming thing, the anger I'd stifled, has been let loose.

I'm still clutching the matchbox. I don't want to keep it. I tuck it under a tussock of grass, where it will bleach and buckle. Maybe a child will find it, and open in surprise to a whiff of salt-wind.

I drive away, I think about my mother's death. My father died many years before. Maybe there was nothing left, between her and the expanse of the land. Between her and the widest streets of town.

I remember her house after she'd gone: empty, yet full, bursting. Flicking through photos; stacks of papers, letters. Bearing the coats and dresses out the door to the op shop. I stood in my mother's kitchen; smelling the smell of her cupboards. The things arranged on the kitchen benches; cuttings in jars of water, rotting.

The fruit that was never eaten. The blue fur on the oranges; the fruit-fly clouds. The fruit that was never eaten. The fridge choked with food with leftovers. Meat, eggs, jars and jars. What to do with this food that no-one can eat?

I'd wondered who she was, my mother, and where she had gone. She had never learnt to drive.

The town releases me, after I have driven for an hour, lost in a wilderness of cul-de-sacs. As I drive out the smell of regret fades, the houses peter out, the scrub takes over. I head toward home, the city that lies far south of here.

Then I remember the rest of the dream. The dream I had back in the motel. I was walking across a vast, stretched-out beach of ribbed sand, crossed by channels of rushing water. Up ahead pools of water reflected the sky, disappeared like mirages as I approached. The sea was far off. Everything was far away-squat people, bright family groups advanced but never came close. Nothing was close. I looked down at the hard, ridged sand-it was like a view from a plane. Then I was descending, over brown and olive paddocks, over the green dead eyes of dams. Dead trees were fragile skeletal hands, reaching out of the deadland.

BEFORE THE WAVE

She comes to me by night, smelling of the briny sea, her body slippery with sea lettuce, garlanded with Neptune's necklace. The room is lit by the green fluorescent numbers on the alarm clock, stuck at 3 am, strobing. In this greenish, flashing light she creeps toward the bed, her face, statue-like after years of being carved by the sea.

Every morning I wake up to sticky sheets and the scent of her in the room. Or is it the sea herself, ever-present behind the shut blinds.

I'd come to the island in the winter, for the quiet. I looked forward to gentle days on uncrowded beaches and a calm sea, still warm enough to swim in. But a wild thing had arrived—a wind stirring everything up, blasting up my memories so that images from the past would appear right in front of me.

I hadn't set foot on the place for years, but after the break-up I needed to get away. I couldn't believe how it'd changed. High-rise apartment blocks gnashed like teeth along the beachfront, coffee shops that served real espresso and boutique restaurants had taken over from the corner chip shops and the general store.

The first blast from the past was the eleventh-floor apartment. I'd chosen it because it was cheap—despite being beachfront, not realising it hadn't been refurbished for years.

Standing on the wide balcony, smoking, I looked out over the palms to the sea. The palms rustled in the wind and glimmered when the sun came out. So far I hadn't seen much sun—most of the time it was hidden by thick, cream and blue cloud.

The palms were different varieties—Bangalow, date, foxtail and coconut. Their tips were yellowed because palms do not like full sun but crave the shade a jungle provides. The palms surrounded a kidney-shaped pool with a pebbly bottom. Arranged round the pool was an array of white plastic outdoor furniture. A sign warned, Do not yell, scream, jump or dive, but the pool area was empty. I looked down on the inviting jelly waters and let the stress drain out of me. The air was humid. I was cloaked in a furry blanket. Now and then a bird chanted monotonously. The sounds of clashing cutlery came from another unit and I imagined someone cutting up and eating a steak.

It was 1995 but the apartment's decor hadn't changed since the mid-seventies. The low ceiling was sand-blasted pebbles, and on the wall was a large pewter plate, pock-marked with supposedly artistic indentations. There was a seventies cane lounge suite and a chunky tan-wood table and chairs. On the wall above the tv console was a framed print of wild horses galloping along a beach, before a stormy sea and blue-black sky. In a corner of the room stood an old cane writing desk, and in its drawers I found a dog-eared pack of Old Maid and a tin of Dominos.

The whole ensemble reminded me of being a kid on summer holidays, of sandy afternoons after days on the beach sitting cross-legged on the floor with my cousins, playing Snap or Monopoly, drinking strawberry-flavoured milk out of little glass bottles, being sunburned and covered with calamine lotion, while the adults sat round the table drinking beer and rustling newspapers, and murmuring about stuff that kids aren't supposed to be listening to, but do, all the time, weaving the stories and phrases into their own games.

It made me feel at home, being in this apartment. The kitchen drawers were stuffed with an assortment of odd cutlery, inside the cupboards were chipped and mismatched plates and cups, and Irish whisky glasses with rhymes on the sides, and a set of mugs that were exactly the same as the ones we had when I was a kid.

The bedroom, at the back of the apartment, was small and dark with one tiny frosted-glass window high up in the rear wall. A king-sized bed took up most of the space. A walk-in closet adjoined the room and a tiny ensuite whose plastic vanity basin of marbled brown and cream contrasted with the bronze edging of the shower cubicle and mirror. A back door led out to a small landing and view of the car-park. I upended my bags on the bed and got into my loose pants and faded Hawaiian shirt.

Down on the beach it seemed windier, the sea the colour of coffee with a little milk stirred into it. Medium-sized, aggressive waves ate at the narrow, sloping beach in cascades of brown-tinged foam. I walked against the wind, the sand blowing up and stinging my face. Still, it was great being away from the city and crowds. I rolled up my pants and waded at the edge of the sea, enjoying the feel of the foam around my ankles and the wet, pappy sand between my toes.

I passed an old couple standing together on the beach strip, the coffee waves groping at their feet. They appeared to be arguing and didn't notice me as I strode past in the stinging wind. They looked to be both in their seventies, white-haired, but fit and slim. The woman was talking at the man and waving her arms, which were gilded with dozens of gold bangles. The man, whose white moustache set off his tan, was staring out at the hungry sea, trying to ignore her. The wind carried off whatever the woman was yelling, so I could not discern her accent, but I guessed that the couple was American, well-heeled American tourists.

Being off-season, most of the shops and restaurants were shut on the beachfront, but I found a fish shop, a remnant from the days of old. I bought cooked prawns wrapped in newspaper and sat on a pier at the end of the beach with my legs dangling. I ate the sweet flesh greedily, even sucking out the gritty brains, and threw the heads and shells into the water.

By the stumps of the pier, in knee-deep water, were two tourists, snorkelling. In their shiny black wet-suits, they resembled crawling beetles. When one of them saw something, he or she would yell out through the snorkel. It came out as a strangled cry. I wondered how come they could see anything in the turbid water. And by the time the other snorkeler had splashed over to see what the other had seen, the fish, or whatever, would surely be long gone. They were snorkelling so shallow I thought they must be scraping their noses on the coral sand.

The amateur snorkelers disgruntled me. I rinsed my hands in the sea, knowing it wouldn't do much good, and that for days the scent of prawn would linger on my fingers, bringing more briny memories. The waves pawed at my ankles, I might have been dragged into deeper channels.

The snorkelers reminded me of early days on the island. I had seen Eagle rays, in clusters, a scattering of brown coins, moving imperceptibly to shore. I remembered snorkelling in glass-clear, pure water. Clouds of tiny fish moved as one body, flashing metallic as they turned. Sweetlip and the Coral Trout, suspended in shafts of sunlight, mouthing like cows. I remember the cold draughts of deeper seas and staring down through endless green where a diver, tiny, yellow and squashed-looking, moved over the sea's floor. I was a cork, bobbing above all that life, the sun on my back.

The next day the sun was out, but the wind had worsened. I walked a long way up the beach, in the opposite direction, looking for a sheltered spot. I passed mansions, half-hidden amongst the remnant she-oaks at the edge of the beach. One of these great homes was a real ostentatious Gone with the Wind style Hollywood production with thick white Roman columns, and a deserted tennis court. I trudged on until there were no more hotels or mansions and found a patch of soft white sand in the crook of a she-oak grove. I pulled off my tee-shirt and plonked down on my towel. This part of the beach curved round like a boomerang, and so was more sheltered from the wind. The tide was out, exposing shimmering mud-flats, and further along were mangroves, cut off from me by an estuary of amber water. It looked like crocodile country, but I knew there were no crocs here. It was sunny and pleasant, despite an occasional sulphurous whiff from the mangroves.

The beach was deserted until a blot further up drew closer and materialised into a jogger—a young man in long shorts, feet pummelling the soft sand. He halted right in front of me, bent over, hands on splayed knees, plump tomato face like a baby's. 'Hey, you got the time?' he brayed in an American accent. I shook my head and he plodded on, a side of beef in a baseball cap, cooked red in the midday sun. I shut my eyes—I wanted to erase him from my memory. There didn't used to be tourists at this time of year, what had happened to the place?

I fell asleep and woke what seemed to be moments later, my body peppered in fine sand and my mouth dry. I leaned up on one elbow. The tide was further out, and way off in the shallow water was a figure, walking. A stick silhouette against the glinting coffee water. The figure strolled, stooped, paused and walked on. Stooped to pick something up, examine it and either drop it into a bucket or discard it. I think it was the way of walking that got my attention. As she got closer and I made out her body-shape, I felt sure it was her. So much so I felt the old fear. I needed to get up and walk away. But I continued to stare at her, unable to move. I watched her stroll across the bay, until she was far away, wading through the estuary and onto the beach on the other side, where she walked until she was out of sight.

It couldn't be her. It was what, twenty years ago? It had to be some local girl. Could've been her daughter. The fear lunged at me-my belly lurched. I leapt up, grabbed my towel and strode up the beach. Halted, because I felt suddenly very anxious for the girl. I turned and squelched through the mud in the direction she'd gone. I couldn't make her out on the beach across from the estuary-she had disappeared.

I was torn between crossing the estuary and seeing if the girl was okay or heading back to the apartment. What if something had happened? I'd seen her out there and didn't do anything to help. At the same time I knew these notions were ridiculous, and I was acting out of anxiety, and past fears. Nevertheless I decided I would check on the girl. It was like when you go back to make sure the door is locked before going to bed, even though you know you locked it half an hour before. That kind of feeling.

The waters of the estuarine creek swept through the mangroves, raging now as it drained out to sea. Its banks, where it crossed the beach, were steep ledges of sand which broke off and fell into the fast flowing water. I would never be able to cross there, and decided instead to walk out over the mud-flats and cross to the other beach that way, avoiding the deeper part of the estuarine channel. I left my sandals on the beach and set off bare-foot, draping my towel across my shoulders to protect myself from the sun, which had intensified despite the lateness of the afternoon.

Out on the flats the sand was criss-crossed by channels of rushing water, washing away shoals of prickly puffer fish, tumbling shells, meaty strips of sea tulips and screw-like shark's eggs. I leapt over the little channels and tried to keep to the hard, ridged sand, but sometimes I would sink knee, or even thigh-deep in sand, which under the surface was black and foul-smelling.

I laboured on, feeling my way, the strong current pulling against my calves and then my thighs as I waded deeper. I wished I had a stick to test the depth of the water ahead of me. The beach across from the estuary was now only a few metres away. I wondered how the girl had gotten over so quickly under these conditions. I was edging forward when I lost my footing altogether. I was caught in a deep channel, being swept out to sea. I panicked, my arms flailing about. My head went under and I swallowed a great gulp of sea-water. I knew there was no-one around to help, and gasping from the shock, allowed myself to be carried along, realizing in the midst of all the chaos, that I was being swept close to the beach on the estuary's opposite side. I felt I had only one chance, and took it, striking out, I was able to scrabble onto the shallows of the beach where the girl had disappeared.

I stretched out on the wet sand, my palms pressing into its hardness. A little sand-coloured crab scuttled past my cheek, paused for a second, and regarded me. If I kept still would it nibble me, thinking I was dead? Soon I'd be covered with them.

There's a point where you stop fighting, when you think, 'I've had enough—just take me.' They say that's how it is, with drowning. They say it's a calm way to die, when you give in to it. At first, there was the beauty of it, the sunlight flashing on acres of froth from the churned-up sea. We easily leapt up and caught the waves before they broke. She was laughing out loud, her giggles swallowed by the sound of waves. Both of us good swimmers, beach kids, used to the sea. We had run past the *Danger: Beware of Rips* sign without even looking at it.

It had not happened on this island, but on a part of the coast near where we lived. We'd taken the bus and wagged school for the day. A group of us, drinking beer and smoking, getting rough and chucking sand at each other.

My girlfriend and I had left the others, and run into the surf. We kept diving under the breakers, talking and laughing when we surfaced. It was when we couldn't touch bottom anymore that we realised we were in trouble. She stretched out her arms to me—but I couldn't reach her, she was too far out. The waves were relentless, breaking over us, sucking us into themselves. Inside a wave, in the rush of foam and green water I thought I saw her, being tumbled about like some doll or dead sea creature. A crab or a fish. I broke the surface and she was nowhere. I struggled in against the current—I had to save myself. Touched bottom at last, and then I was on the beach, vomiting sea-water. She was nowhere. Some of the others had run back up the beach, about two ks it was—to the patrolled area, to get the lifesavers.

I eased myself up from the sand, exhausted, my head pounding. The only way back was through the mangroves— there's no way I could get back the way I'd come. The mangrove forest adjoined the main road and after a while I emerged, bitten by sand flies, sunburnt and windburnt. I trudged barefoot, home to the apartment.

It was after my near-drowning experience that the dreams began. Each night she'd visit me, in the room's greenish light. We were underwater, struggling together inside a wave, rolling weightless to some other purpose. Perhaps I was drunk on sea-water, delirious from an overdose of sun and wind. In the morning I'd wake shivering in soaked sheets.

Before the wave that drew us apart, before the wave that took her. In that space of time. The dunes laced with pigface, the sagging wire fence. The deep white sand squeaked under our feet as we ran to the sea. Her skin was brown and coated in a sheen of powdery sand. Giggling, ribbing each other. In that space of time, as we stepped into cool water, she scooped up handfuls of foam and threw them to the wind. The waves sucked at our calves, our thighs, in that space of time, the sun glinted on foam acres. The beauty of it.

Back at the apartment I avoid the bedroom and fall into a paralysed sleep on the cane lounge. After a couple of hours I wake, still tired but with a hunger. It's early evening and the sky's slashed with neon lipstick. I head along the esplanade looking for a shop or restaurant that's open, and there's the old couple I'd seen, strolling toward me, their white clothes shining in the fading light. They are arm in arm, she a little ahead, seeming to lead the old man. As they get closer she addresses me in a strong Southern American accent, that reminds me of Blanche in A Streetcar Named Desire, 'Where's the Barrier Reef?'

There is no lead-up to it, no 'Hello, how are you', or 'Terrible weather, isn't it?' Just a demand of someone who looks Australian and might be a local.

'Out there.' I wave toward the open sea, irritated by their rudeness and prepared to keep walking. But the couple are right in front of me now, barring my way. Her lipstick, bright red, has been drawn outside her lip's boundaries. Her doll head bobbles a little above a hollow neck. She points at the sea, the gold bangles clang. 'Have you been out there?'

'Of course.' I try to assert my local status. 'Years ago. It's bleached, the coral. It isn't as good now, to look at.'

'Ye see, Carson?' she turns to her husband, and pats the huge knuckles of his old, freckled hand. 'Ye see? It's no good anymore.'

But the old man is looking past us, staring out to sea, and muttering under his breath. She turns back to me. 'Carson here isn't himself. Ever since we got to the island, he's acting real nervous. All he can talk about is the reef. But they won't let us go on account of the bad weather conditions. He won't let up, though. I'm real worried about him.'

I watch the couple stroll on, arm in arm, the woman leading. Every now and then, the elderly fellow turns to look back at the sea. They head toward the newer, more up-market apartment block next door to mine.

I find a restaurant that's open and I'm escorted to a courtyard, lush with tropical plants. The waitress is a local high-school student who smiles when I try to engage her in conversation. Tables of rough wood have benches for seats and on each is a tea-light candle in a frosted glass holder. The little flames flicker. I'm the only customer.

I pick the Catch of the Day and when it arrives it's a whole parrot fish, blue and orange, garlanded with tired parsley, resplendent on an porcelain platter. The fish's colours are fading, its greenish-blue beak slightly open, as if in mild surprise. The pupil of its wide round eye is a little off-centre, as though the fish is looking askance at me. 'I don't know if I can eat this,' I say to the waitress. 'It's too beautiful.'

The waitress, in an orange sundress of tropical pattern and a frangipani over her ear, hovers at the side of my table, and says flatly, 'Would you like me to remove the head, Sir?'

I stare at the fish and would not be surprised if it were to open its parrot beak and speak to me. I dismiss the waitress, try to rally my manly self. I poke the fish with my fork and peel off a little flesh. I am still staring at it when the waitress returns with a little bowl of wilted, yellowed salad.

I give up, and call for the bill, the fish wins. On my way out I notice the large lit aquarium in which a dozen reef fish huddle in a corner, fins drooping.

I haven't left the apartment in the past few days. I sleep late, exhausted, tangled in sheets. The chug of the air conditioner blots out the sound of the sea. The apartment block seems deserted, though late last night I heard the sounds of someone moving furniture around on the floor above me. It went on for hours, then stopped, just when I was about to look for a broom to thump on the ceiling.

I'd stocked the fridge with beer of all kinds—Australian brands and some of the more up-market German ones. In the late afternoons I sit out on the balcony drinking. The wrought iron Queen Anne chairs are uncomfortable and leave a pattern on your bum. There is a wrought iron Queen Anne table to go with the chairs. On the table is a small pair of binoculars that I'd brought with me, thinking I might spend time idly observing passing ships or sea birds.

She was a couple of grades below me at school and I persuaded a girl I knew, who was kind of a friend, to ring her up and let her know I was interested. The whole thing was really embarrassing. Although it paid off in the end because I finally got to know her and then it was like we were going together. It's fairly unpleasant sitting out here today. The warm wind comes in blasts and the palms sound like those strings of flapping plastic flags they hang over car-yards.

The closest we ever got to having sex was lying together and kissing on the double bed of the parents of a girlfriend. The girl's parents were away for a weekend and she'd invited all of her friends over on a Saturday afternoon. When we finally came out of the room adjusting our clothes everyone was silent and stared at us because they thought we'd actually had sex on my friend's parents' bed. I remember the dress she was wearing—one of those bright patterns, a paisley. Through the silky material I'd felt her breast, and through it the pulse of her heart.

I worry about locking myself out on the balcony because if you shut the sliding glass door behind you, it automatically locks. And usually I do shut the sliding glass door because I don't want the wind blowing through the apartment. I always try to make sure I have a key in my pocket when I come out here. I wonder what would happen if I got shut out. I certainly wouldn't be able to climb onto the next apartment's balcony because I'm scared of heights, and as there doesn't seem to be too many people around, I don't like my chances if I had to yell for help Although I suppose someone would hear me. The girl whose house it was ran into the room and checked her parents' flawless chenille bedspread for stains. The dried-out palm leaves lash and dance. As they bend, I catch glimpses of the sea, greyish and furled in white-caps. No ships.

Every afternoon the overweight tourist who I saw jogging on the beach pounds past along the footpath adjacent to the apartments. If I was locked out I could call out to him, although he'd be sure not to hear me because he's plugged into his Walkman. I watch him through the binoculars, his face shiny and flesh juddering. Susan had said that part of the reason she wanted to separate was because I was never really present, she said it was like trying to relate to someone who was on the other side of one of those rice-paper screens they use in Japanese houses. Shadow-man. She called me that once. I take a slug of beer. I haven't eaten today. My stomach has grown in the past days, from all the beer. I pat the gut that's bulging above my fly.

A sudden loud knocking sound causes me to feel for the key in my shorts' pocket. I stand for a moment, unsure of where it's coming from, until I realise it's someone pounding on the apartment door.

The banging goes on as I run through the apartment and fling the door open. It's her again, the elderly American woman in white. Like last time, there is no preamble. 'You a doctor.' she shouts at me. 'They said at reception you was a doctor.'

'They said I was a doctor?' I bark out a laugh. My own voice sounds so strange to me since I haven't spoken to anyone for several days. She follows me through to the lounge room and we stand at either side of the tan-wood table. I realise my chin is rough with four o'clock shadow and I'm still wearing the sweat-stained tee-shirt I put on several days ago. I see that she is very agitated, her lively hands jangling their gold manacles.

'I'm not a medico, if that's what you mean. I'm a PhD.'

The old lady frowns, she looks for a minute like she's smelled something bad. I've been mistaken for a medical doctor on two other occasions. Once during a concert, when a young woman fainted, and once when a neighbour's kid was bitten by a dog. Only on the first occasion did I play along.

'It's Carson,' says the old lady. 'He needs help. His nerves are real bad. He's still going on about this reef thing. Thelma, he says to me, we just gotta see the reef. Won't eat. It's like he's on another planet. And I can't get us off this damn island—due to the weather.'

I move over to the kitchen bench, pour Thelma a brandy, throw in some ice and hand it over. Then I pour myself one to keep her company.

She takes a sip and looks a bit calmer, like something's drained out of her. It must be pretty tiring looking after Carson, keeping him out of trouble. She reminds me of my mother. And the old guy's a bit like dad was—distracted, in a world of his own. Maybe I could be of help. I did a couple of psych subjects at uni.

I pull out a chair for her and she sinks onto it. She looks exhausted.

'We'd always wanted to come out to Australia,' she drawls, 'but it's not what we thought. This island, it's not like the pictures in the magazines. And the weather's terrible.'

Wind bashes at the balcony door, as though to emphasise her point.

'But I don't mind all that. It's what's happening to Carson that I can't stand.'

I try to be comforting. I put a concerned expression on my face. In the back of my mind something's nagging at me. It's hard to concentrate on what she's saying. We sip our brandies.

She sighs. 'It's good to talk to someone. I don't know who Carson is anymore.'

After a while she says, 'You here alone?'

I tell her my wife, Susan, left me. That I'm having a break, on my own. No, I tell her, there's no kids. Thank goodness.

She looks me up and down, takes in my chin stubble. 'Well, you look like you could do with a little mothering.'

I shrug it off. 'Nah, it's the weather. It'd get on anyone's nerves.'

She finishes her glass and we both stand. 'I feel better,' she announces.

'It's just a matter of waiting it out—the storm.' I say.

She is in the middle of murmuring her thanks when something thumps against the balcony's glass sliding door. I open to a puddle of blood on the concrete floor and a fearful seagull staring up at us. 'Oh the poor thing.' exclaims Thelma, who is pushing past me and advancing on the wounded bird. But the seagull is having none of it and hops to the far end of the balcony.

We both look up at once. The light has gone queer, everything is bathed in an apricot luminosity. Seabirds, blown before the storm, shine like confetti. On the horizon is a great swathe of grey jelly cloud. It flaps toward us like a solid thing. As we retreat into the apartment it grows larger by the second. I slam shut the sliding doors and pull the blinds.

We look into each other's panicked faces. The wrought iron furniture is scraping across the balcony.

Everything is happening at once. Carson, tossing in his bed, is treading water toward a shimmering, jewelled reef laced with coral in popsicle colours. Down at the jetty, tourists waiting for a ferry, abandon their suitcases and backpacks and stumble backwards into the pandanus.

'What is it? What is it?' Thelma screeches into my face. I try to stop her returning to Carson but it's no use, the white blouse rips in my hands as she makes for the door.

As the glass doors shatter and the blinds smash I can feel her. I stumble into the bedroom and know she is waiting. As the wave crashes into the apartment, in the confusion of churning water and busted furniture, I feel her grasp my hand.

MENACE

I woke out of dreams to see you standing by the bed. You were in your white shirt that looked like a nightdress, but of course it wasn't a nightdress, it's not your style. It was during the fire season. The exhausted night shrieked with insects.

My feet were wound up in the sheet; I was paralysed. I couldn't speak. You whispered, 'Look there', and pointed out the window. I sat up and saw it—the lights, the spotlights bouncing in the trees, and I could hear it, realised I'd heard it all along, roaring in my dreams, the careening vehicles trammelling our fences.

'We're not safe,' you said. You'd been saying that since we'd arrived. You'd said the feeling was to do with the empty spaces, the aching bareness of the place. The dead trees like old bone, poking at the rounded sky. You feared it, you'd said. If you died out here, the country would not know or care. The crows would settle on you and pick out your jelly eyes. And yet you loved it, that country.

I got out of bed and pulled on my jeans. The curtains were open and we ducked when the spotlights illuminated the rooms. They were closer, they were circling the house. Under the roar of engines I could hear their whoops and yells. Looking back, it seemed as if we were crouched together on the lino for hours, in the dark, our heads down, clinging on to each other, the lights flashing. Then it went quiet.

We left at the end of the two years, we flew out over that country. Over the spines of mountains, over the milky eyes of dams. Over the spent country where we had left our rural fantasies.

We returned to the city. I asked you if you felt safe at last. You said we aren't safe here either. There's menace in the air. But we are anonymous here, you said. The soft city, it absorbs you. Out there we were exposed against the hard ground.

In the city, it hasn't stopped raining. A different house, a different place. We moved in a few months ago. Here, the sky is white, glaring beyond the windows, broken by the strokes of the power lines, wavy lines in the old glass, a child's drawing of electricity. Outside, the wet road is opening its pores, baring itself.

The house reminds us of a ship, its sharp triangular front yard, the prow. It is a ship moored on the street, ready to advance.

Under the roar of rain we feel protected. I pace from room to room looking out of windows. In the room at the front of the house, under the bay windows, where a chaise longue should go, is a large fish-tank. The fish glide through ribbon weed or hover in groups, under cascades of bubbles.

There are small triangular-shaped fish whose enamelled bodies shine in rainbow colours as they flit and catch the light, and ground-dwellers, gudgeons, with mauvish speckled flesh, like an old bruise. The gudgeons do not move often, but like to prop themselves on rocks and survey their world. When they do move they are fast. They flick off with grumpy, impatient strokes, scattering pebbles. There is one large gudgeon, an old one. Her colours have faded; her body has grown awkward and stiff. She belonged to us before we went up north. We left her with a friend who gave her back to us when we returned to the city. We set up the large tank to accommodate this old fish.

You and I sit on cushions on the floor watching the fish. The old fish appears from behind the rocks and regards us. Her gills quiver. You rap with your nails on the glass and she comes toward you. She gets excited, thinking she's going to be fed, wriggles up the side of glass showing her silver belly.

Things were going on up there before anything major happened, I say. Hard to prove because it wasn't out in the open. People were talking behind my back. I had a feeling about it—rather than knowing what was going on. Like at work one day. I walked in late and they didn't know I was there. I was getting mail out of my pigeon-hole and I could hear the others out in the staff room uproariously laughing. One of them was telling a joke—something about fish—a cunnilingus joke—I caught the tail end of it. Then I heard someone say my name. I knew then that they knew. Shortly after that the blokes in the utes came over.

You didn't tell me about the work stuff at the time, you say.

I didn't want to worry you, I say.

I don't say to you that at the time I felt ashamed. It's hard to tell you these things. The way they think about us, the way they see us, makes me want to hide.

When it rained up there, you say, when it finally rained after months of drought, it belted down on the hard ground. It exposed things—the buried things—the teeth and bones of creatures that had died starving, eating dust. I felt like that, you say. A little bundle of picked-clean bones exposed in the middle of a paddock.

We had nowhere to hide. We crouched on the floor in the middle of the house. In the silence we waited. Then we heard the first rock crash on the tin roof. We heard their laughter and yells. They sounded pissed. The crescendo on the roof came like a hailstorm. Instinctively we ducked down, our arms over our heads. In the moment of silence that followed, you stood. You were breathless, shaking. You said you were going out there—you'd tell them to piss off. I clung onto you—you can't go—it's too dangerous.

When things went awry up there they blamed the weather. People went mad in that heat, troppo. And there were the fires. We had been watching the fires in the hills at the back of the property. We stood together in the kitchen, at night, with the lights off, looking out at the patterns of flame on the hillside. The fire was far away, not really part of us. The fire-line grew outwards, in ever-widening circles. By day, the blue sky was smudged by grimy fingers. Burnt leaves, carried on the wind, fluttered down on us.

Those hills were a no-man's land. I climbed up there once. Shallow-rooted trees twisted themselves out of rock. The chant of cicadas was deafening. Down on the plain our house roof glared out of the bitten-back land.

The house was thirty kilometres out of town. No neighbours. We rented it off a cow-cocky who lived on the other side of the property. We worked in the town and at the university. The town was a cattle town. On the way in the road went past the meatworks. A horseman would shut the gate across the road so cattle could be driven from the yards to the abattoir. People sat in their cars and waited, watching the blur of hides go through the race in a haze of dust. In the town, the shadows of the jacaranda trees leaned out across the baking streets. You said you could always smell the yellow, choppy river, over-hung with the scent of manure and straw.

Scattered around town were the statues of bulls. All the major breeds were represented: Santa Gertrudis, Brahman, Hereford. A student placed a large pair of fibreglass wings on one of them, and painted its testicles red. It was to commemorate the first slaughter of the year at the meatworks. The local council wasn't impressed. The student was charged with vandalism and the council workers had to remove the wings and the paint before anyone had a chance to see or take a photo.

We were back in the city when we read in the paper about Matthew Shepard—the gay student who was murdered in Wyoming. How he'd been hit eighteen times in the head with a gun butt. How he was kicked over and over in the groin. How he was lashed to the paddock fence so tight they couldn't cut the rope. The cyclist who found him thought he was a scarecrow. At that stage he was still alive. He'd been tied up there for eighteen hours. His head was covered in blood—except for a clean spot 'where he'd been crying and tears went down his face.'

Wyoming. A place I'd dreamt of as a child. A wide-open place. Prairies and big skies.

In this house in the city I feel hemmed-in, closed in by the rain. Outside the sky is darkening and lights are coming on in houses. I slide up the window and smell crushed snails and wet vegetation. The street is empty of people. Cars burn round the corner.

I feel you behind me, somewhere in the dim room. You ask if I believe in the existence of evil. I tell you I continue to believe what I've always believed: everything is socially constructed, people act in certain ways due to social and historical forces. We have had this conversation many times before. I do not believe as you do, that evil is an independent force existing in the ether—that one taps into it or is entrapped by it. You say you understand the social constructs but that you see evil as intrinsic to life, a part of us.

I say that up there, anything could have happened. There was a climate of intolerance. Pauline Hanson made it worse. Her comments about Aboriginal people getting more money, that Australia was in danger of being swamped by Asians—it bolstered prejudices about minorities, it fanned up fear.

By the way, you say, the roof is leaking. In the bedroom you show me the line of drips along a crack in the ceiling.

That night the hoons came in their utes, we wanted to make ourselves invisible. We felt the hard floor under our limbs, and wished we could sink into it, through the lino and wooden boards, to the netherworld of under the house, into a bolt-hole of dust and cobwebs. Their lights traversed the room, floated over our faces. We screwed up our faces, hid them in our hands. We did not want to see their dark forms at the window, leering in at us.

We stayed put until we heard them drive off. Outside, the hot night shrieked with the police-whistle bands of insects. You walked up the driveway to padlock the gate. It was there you found their calling-card.

A dead fish, hung on the gate. Your torch caught its flat eye. Its guts were slit and dripped foul liquid. You knocked it off the gate with a stick and batted it into the bushes.

This room is filled with the sounds of bubbling air-stones and gushing filters. The old fish is flirting with her mate, a gudgeon less than half her size. Fins erect, gills puffed out, the two fish perform a kind of dance, tail to fin. They twine around and around each other. He smooths his head along her side, his spots brightening to intense crimson. Their play has an edge of danger—she could take off his head with one bite.

There's a break in the rain. We walk in the nearby park, in the dusk, over sodden grass where black mud has risen. The paths are draped in skeins of drowning earthworms, lustrous under park-lights.

I slide my hand into the crook of your elbow, and leave it there. In the dusk, in the soft city, no-one remarks on us.

A building wavers at the park's edge, a hotel. Art Deco style, hung with coloured lights that are blurred in the misty air. We are drawn toward it. We stand looking in through its glowing porthole windows. It could be an ocean liner, stranded in the rain, washed up at the park's edge. Inside, we see creatures, half-fish, half-human, play, dance and manoeuvre pool cues. Their webbed fingers gesticulate. Their hair is stiffened into iridescent points. Their scaly skins are cross-hatched in rainbow colours. We watch, fascinated, and tentatively step forward.

EARTH EATERS

Mum had said I was to go up there, to *Margot*. Sherrie was on her own. I was fifteen, had finished grade ten and was supposed to start work at the newsagent's. I wanted to go to Sherrie's, to get away from Mum, especially from her voice that had become high and toneless and sounded distant even if you were standing right next to her.

My sister was older. She became a mother to me, and Tom was the father I never had. We three were a family, in those first months at *Margot*.

We shared out the precious water, bathing in each other's dirt. Once a week you were allowed to fill the bath-tub, knuckle-deep, and sit in tepid, mud-coloured water.

We spent a lot of time in the kitchen, joking 'round the table, above a jumble of food, sauce bottles, old women's magazines. Sherrie wavered between sink and stove, pinned nylon shorts hugging her brown legs.

Tom was always fiddling or carving, doing things with his fingers, his red hands, thick and square, nails bitten-down to little squares. In the first few months he was so often joking, laughing, teasing, but I saw that his face was distracted at times, worry flickering across it. He'd grab her round the waist, knead at her sides, they'd be smooching and I'd look away, out to the hills, the summer fires in the air, tightening my throat.

They were sweet-hearts, always holding hands and kissing and cuddling. When we went to town, shopping, Sherrie would reach up for a can of peas and Tom would be right there behind her, his hands on her waist. And she'd swing around, and they'd be staring at each other and smiling, her still holding up the can of peas.

I was embarrassed to be around them. They'd be all over each other in the supermarket, touching each other, wheeling the shiny trolley between them, throwing in tinned bully-beef, packets of jelly crystals, tuna, tomato sauce, spaghetti, clang clang. Things to fill the pantry shelves, to clutter up the table. Jars for Tom to twist open, screwing up his face.

We were finishing a meal of frizzled chops when Tom turned to me and said, 'She had a lot of boyfriends, didn't she, Nat?' and winked at me.

I dropped the chop-bone I'd been gnawing. 'Yeah, heaps. Lots of them coming over all the time.'

Tom chuckled.

'No, I didn't Nat,' said Sherrie primly. 'There was only that bloke, Bob. He was the only one before Tom, you know that.'

'That's not really true, is it Nat?' asked Tom, red-faced, turning to me and grinning.

'That's right,' I laughed, through a mouthful of juicy fat. 'There were so many boyfriends, I lost count.'

Sherrie rose with a scrape of her chair and took our plates from us, scooping the scraps from the remains of our meal into an old chewed ice-cream container to give to Banjo. As she moved around the kitchen the floorboards under her bare feet screeched and squawked.

'Just how many boyfriends did she have?' boomed Tom, addressing the room in general.

Sherrie crashed the plates down in the sink and spun around. 'You know, Natalie, I didn't have any boyfriends except Bob. So stop lying about it.' Her voice had gotten that shrill edge and tears glittered in her eyes. Tom nudged my arm and grinned at me with bared white teeth.

'There was only Bob,' said Sherrie, 'you know that, Tom.'

She came at us and wrenched the table cloth up from under our elbows. Tom put his booted foot up on the table. Sherrie flung a tea towel at me. 'You can dry up. And you can put your feet down, Tom.'

There was silence, punctuated by the clattering of plates and cutlery. Tom eased his leg back down, but sat, picking at his dirty nails with a matchstick. 'Who was this Bob fellow then, Nat? Some cowboy?'

I dried the dishes and didn't say another word. I could feel Sherrie brisk and tense beside me.

Most nights after dinner we went to our rooms—theirs was across the hall from mine. The generator hummed for a couple of hours until Tom shut it down. With the winding down of the generator, all the lights blinked on and off, then all cut out at once. I would fling down the book or magazine I'd been reading and lie in the darkness, listening to the night sounds, the insect chorus, the drumming of toads and the beasts in the paddock, bellowing out to each other across the grasslands.

I would hear the sounds from across the hall: the crying, laughing, shouting, cursing, coming from behind their bedroom door. I felt their room would explode and fly apart unable to contain it all. Their voices bellowed on in my dreams.

Bob had come to our house one Sunday when Mum was out. He was in the army, Sherrie had said. He tumbled out of a carload of blokes, all waving fists and flailing arms, and whoo-whooing out the windows. The car skidded round our front drive; I stood with my bike as the gravel flew. Bob's hair was crew-cut. I wondered what it would feel like to touch. As he walked past, I watched the dance of greenish-blue tats on the plump muscle of his upper arm. I followed Sherrie and Bob into the house. Sherrie turned on me . 'Why don't you go out for a while?' she asked, pressing five dollars into my hand.

I was twelve then and still in love with my bike, an old rusty thing with loose, rattling mud-guards. I rode up and down the glaring gravel roads that surrounded the blocks of the new housing estate where we lived. Most of the houses hadn't been built and empty slabs lay stark amongst mounds of earth and rocks. When the brand new houses went up, before the families claimed them, us kids stared through the uncurtained windows at the naked rooms, at the rolls of underfelt and kitchens with handle-less cupboards. A boy broke all the windows in a new house and was sent to juvenile detention.

I headed back to our house but Sherrie came out to meet me as I peddled up the drive. She was flushed, her fair hair frizzed up, and I saw that the fly-button on her jeans was undone.

'You haven't been gone very long,' she said. 'Why don't you go for another ride?'

I stood my ground. 'I'm thirsty.'

'Wait here, then.'

She strode inside the house and hurried back out with a cup of cold cordial. She waited while I gulped it down. 'Now, go,' she commanded. 'Remember I gave you five bucks.'

I turned the bike and wheeled away. I rode all the way out to the rubbish tip and stared into the smouldering trench where swollen black plastic seethed with maggots and could've hidden a body. Black crows flapped through the lantana—their yellow eyes accusing. I threw down the bike and smashed some bottles, until I heard a car rattle up.

When I got home it was dusk. Mum had been worried and yelled at me when I came in the door. Sherrie sat at the kitchen table. 'Was it enough time,' I whispered, 'to do what you wanted to do?' She just stared at me.

*

I got to know *Margot*. I got to know Tom. Moody. He would just ignore me sometimes. Other times he'd laugh and joke, tell stories about visiting *Margot* as a boy. How the green frogs upholstered the house-stumps and water lay for months on the plain, bringing flocks of birds, even a regal pair of pelicans. He told stories about dogs and horses he'd had. His great grandfather's dog Jock was a border collie with one white eye and one blue. It fought snakes, even a deadly taipan once, but died of a tick found too late, latched to its inner lip.

Stories about the people, the army camping out on *Margot* during the war, the prospectors sifting the gullies for gold, the Aborigines marched through *Margot* in chains.

Tom spoke of the cattle, knew them all individually, and the mob of half-wild horses, a *Margot* breed. There was a bit of Arab in them, Tom said. 'Good doers', they lived on lily-shoots in the dams when feed was scarce. They avoided humans and it took half a day to round them up and catch them. They were unshod but their hoofs were hard and accustomed to the dry plains of *Margot*. Their manes grew long and were tangled with burrs and their ragged tails dragged the ground.

'Tom keeps to himself,' said Sherrie. But there were times when even he could not do it all alone. One dawn I looked out to see two men unloading their horses, a melee of dogs round their feet.

The men were invited to breakfast. One was short and stocky, sausage arms flew out from a seemingly shoulderless body. The other was older, thin and tall with a grey, knotted beard and a guttural accent I couldn't decipher. They removed their hats and sat stiffly in the bright kitchen while Sherrie thumped round, frying eggs, bread, sausages and chops.

Tom's grey horse had a habit of throwing up her head, sometimes so high she'd been known to hit her rider in the face. She had a thick, muscular neck and dainty head. Her black eyes were rimmed with white, giving her a wild look. After he mounted and squeezed her sides she began to mince sideways, rhythmically tossing her head, until he wrenched down with sharp jerks on the reins. Each time she tossed, he jerked in response, until the mare shook her ears in frustration. She ground at the bit, bloody foam bubbling. Tom turned and grimaced at Sherrie, kicked the mare in her sides so that she bounded forward and cantered off. Sweat was already streaming on Tom's horse when the party headed up the paddock, exhilarated dogs fanning out in front.

Sherrie pressed my shoulders, 'She always acts up like that at first. She'll be right once they get going.' I knew she was trying to reassure herself.

'Don't you see', I said, 'he likes her to muck up so he can show off to you.'

'That horse is a bitch,' said Sherrie, 'I'd like to shoot her.' But I caught her hiding her smile.

In a day of blazing sun, Sherrie and I helped work the yarded cattle, beating and prodding the beasts through the race. They would plunge into a trench of insecticide and, bellowing and terrified, swim through the dark liquid, the smell of chemicals and fear rising around us.

The young cattle felt their first, excruciating pain at the hands of men. They were tussled to the ground and branded, then their horns were wrenched off, so that their heads pulsed fountains of bright blood. The young bulls were castrated— the pink meat cut out of the ball sacs and thrown to the frantic, gobbling dogs.

*

Heartbreak country. Everything was sweet, then everything changed.

Tom and Sherrie tried to hide the fights. Slamming around in their room at night. Trying to contain it all. It was bound to bust out one day.

There was a big fight. I'd come back from walking and couldn't find them anywhere. The door to their bedroom stood open wide, showing the large bed with its used, pocked-marked sheet. I wondered about the two of them making love, and found it unimaginable. There was a feeling in the house-the air was charged, as though something had happened-an event that left an invisible, excited residue.

A rifle-crack resounded, hurtled through my body. I pounded out to the verandah, thinking Tom must've shot that python that was eating the chooks. But looking out, there they were, Sherrie and Tom, out on the lawn, eye-balling each other, frozen. Tom had the gun. He was holding it across his body like a shield and poking the muzzle at his own face. She squatted before him, her arms outstretched, fingers splayed. Their red faces held wrinkled grotesque expressions of fear, hate. Their teeth were clenched, tears clung to their eye-rims. Their faces had been remoulded in a few seconds into something alien, evil, other-worldly.

In these moments I noticed everything: the cracked collar of Tom's soft old flannelette shirt, the delicacy of Sherrie's long, articulate fingers, the pinkness of her nails; the scuffed brown bindi-grass, and how quiet everything had become-even the Friar birds were silent in the tulip trees.

Then into the silence, Sherrie poured out a sound that was half-screech, half-howl that ripped at my guts. As she screamed Tom jabbed the rifle at his own cheek.

I fled in slow-motion through the house, looking for somewhere to hide. I thought about that family down south, that we read about in the papers. The father went mad and shot his wife and all the kids. I lay under my bed, listening, waiting for the creak of the floorboards, Tom's footsteps as he came to get me. I listened to the wind, to the dismal clanking of warped metal. After a while I rolled out, brushed off dust and fluff, and crept out to the verandah to see what they were up to.

I could see the bright splotches of their clothes as they tacked to and fro about the paddock. I could hear their distant yelling voices, though I couldn't make out the words. The rest of the afternoon passed that way, with the two of them striking poses of aggression or fear, a series of friezes, in the paddock or house-yard. Slowly, my fear turned to boredom, and I sat leaning against the jacaranda, straining to hear what they were fighting about.

Tom came marching past me, heading for the house. He was bright red-the reddest man I'd ever seen, and he was crying, which shocked me, as I had never seen a man cry before. I did not know that men cried. Sherrie followed close behind and it was she who held the rifle this time. A wretched, shivering Banjo emerged from under the house, tail curled up under his body. The dog stared after the humans, then turned and crept back under.

'Sherrie, what are you doing?' I called out to her. 'I thought you loved each other?'

'You don't know the half of it,' she yelled back over her shoulder.

I watched her humped back as she followed Tom. It was like their hatred held them in a bond as close as their love did. Her hair hung like string. I wondered at their secrets. I was living with these people and knew nothing about them. But Sherrie was my sister-I had thought I knew her as I knew myself.

Tom entered the house and then appeared at the louvres. Behind the rippled glass he was like a man who was drowning, with his blurred underwater face, his gobbling mouth.

I strode out to the paddocks, no longer caring if they killed themselves. It was as though they had reverted to being little kids-I was the only mature one. Then I thought, maybe this is what people do when they are married.

A tame cow separated herself from the herd and strolled up to me. I scratched the indentation between her eyes and the itchy spots behind her ears. She shook her head and chewed her cud. She had been a poddy-calf, hand-reared, and had no fear of humans. I was sorry that I had no treats for her but didn't want to go back to the house to get some. I picked the fat blue ticks from her back and gathered them onto a fence post, then punctured them, one by one, with a sharp dry grass-stalk and watched the ooze of treacle blood.

At dusk I headed with slow steps back to the house, wondering what I would find there. It was quiet except for the hum of the generator and warm lights glowed. Sherrie and Tom appeared at the top of the stairs with their arms around each other, smiling. They were all lovey-dovey again as though nothing had happened. But Sherrie took me aside, held me by the shoulders and said: 'Promise not to tell anyone what happened? Not Mum, or anyone?'

'I promise,' I said.

In the days that followed, the clouds came, teasing us. They were swirls of thick blue cream. I wanted to take my cup and furrow those clouds across the sky. At dusk the cormorants and spoonbills stood high in the dead trees. Pythons dropped out of the tulip trees and slithered under the house. Frogs coughed in the downpipes. We heard the strangled cries of those that were swallowed by the snakes. We waited for rain. We would often stop what we were doing and squint up, waiting for the first fat drops.

Tom killed a goat and we ate its liver just an hour after it died. I watched him slit its throat. The death was so quick. One minute there was a live goat and then just a carcass and red hole. Tom cut up the meat and we bagged it. Banjo carried off the head, holding it delicately by its hair. A goat head that stared with yellow eyes.

The water in the big dam receded, leaving a stretch of deep grey mud. An old cow got stuck-it happened if they weren't strong enough. She had stood, probably all night, and the next day we found her, belly-deep, stretching out her long neck and lowing, fear flicking in her dark eyes. Tom, cursing, waded in and ploughed toward her, roped her up and dragged her out with the tractor. She lay on the bank, paralysed, unable to kick or move her stiff cold legs. He dragged her further, to some shade, and left her there.

I brought her buckets of water from the dam that she sucked greedily up. I fanned the flies off her with a spray of leaves. I rubbed her legs, massaged them, but they were cold and dead.

At dusk I continued to sit with the cow. She lay, resigned, in a cloud of gnats, nibbling at the hay I'd brought her. Tom drove up and stood on the track, and watched me rub the old cow's legs. His face was pale in the fading light. 'Tea's ready,' he said simply.

'Won't do any good,' he gestured toward the cow's dead legs.

'Won't you give her another day? Please? I'll camp out with her tonight.'

Banjo leapt off the back of the ute and rushed at the cow that startled, and tried to struggle up. I held my breath, hoping she would somehow stand. The dog lapped excitedly at the green shit that oozed out of her as she rolled from side to side.

Tom charged toward us and kicked at the kelpie, who scrambled away from us, yelping even though he wasn't hit. Tom grabbed my wrists and pulled me away from the cow. He had never touched me before. He dragged me to the car, pushed me against the door and stood back, breathing heavily. In the fading light I could not see the paleness of his eyes or the boiled redness of his face but there was something about him, a fear mixed with rage. Whatever was between us now had nothing to do with the cow that lowed and stank in the background.

I felt his hand slide under my clothes. I did not move or say anything. His rough, dirty hand cupped my mound and

I felt a tingling, a twisting in my guts. He put one finger in, just the tip, and held it there.

He did not say a word. He held me with the tip of his finger. I didn't move and neither did he. I looked straight ahead, at his freckled chest and the fuzz of hair above his shirt. I listened to his breathing, and to the currawongs dropping pure notes into the early evening. The light was fading out of things, draining out. The old cow shifted, beyond us in her misery.

At last he withdrew. Grim-mouthed, he opened the creaking heavy door of the ute and shuffled me in. I sat smelling the ute's scent of diesel and Tom's sweat. Tom hopped in the driver's side and manoeuvred the ute so the headlights illuminated the paralysed cow. He slid out the rifle from behind the seat. I shut my eyes. The shot, when it came, was a slap. I felt as though I was falling. I opened my eyes to see it was over.

Driving back up the track he reached over and put his hand on my knee. I looked down at the hand and wondered what to do with it. His hand moved higher, over my thigh, which he stroked softly, distractedly. I couldn't think; I sat dumbly. I excused myself at dinner and went to my room.

'She's upset about the cow,' I heard Tom tell Sherrie.

I lay listening to the kitchen sounds, of knives and forks chinking on plates, the washing-up sounds. I listened to the creaking floorboards as they prepared to go to bed. I slept, and then woke sometime in the middle of the night with a raging hunger. I opened the door of the kero fridge and peered inside the dark interior. My fingers felt the pile of pork sausages. I pulled one off the string and held it. Is this what it's like? I thought. Is this what it would feel like, this cold, pink sausage. Then I squeezed hard so the meat erupted out through the end.

THE CRADLE ARMS OF STRANGERS

We always prayed for rain. The monsoonal rains that used to sweep in from the north in the summer, never came. There was one short, bombastic burst. A hard rain that crashed over us and gurgled in our down-pipes for a day and a night. Under the iron roof the din was frightening, like a babble of voices.

Me and Sherrie stood at the louvres and watched the house-yard turn to a brown pool. We had to shout to hear ourselves above the racket. I thought about the family, camping out on our land. Sherrie must've thought the same thing. 'I wonder if that mob will be washed away,' she yelled, and laughed.

But we did not give too much thought to the family. We threw back our heads and breathed deeply of the smell of wet vegetation. Then we ran outside, like children, and played and danced and pushed each other over until we were sodden.

The rain blanked out the hills at the edge of the farm; it encased us in the drumming house. 'For many nights afterwards, across the lawn, frogs sounded as if they were in a slow and never-ending game of ping-pong.

The ground had become too hard to absorb the rain. Water washed uselessly over it, without refreshing the roots of grass or trees. But the rain revived our tanks; it put water in the dam.

Winter was on its way now. The days had shortened. The light was changed. Objects stood out in sharp focus. Every tree, every bush, seemed lit from within. The sky was swishy with mares' tails.

At dusk the paddocks darkened, but the sky above was lit like tv. The still filigrees of dead trees were like cobwebs against the bright sky. The sky turned green at the horizon, and a midnight blue above. The dark shapes of possums scrambled through the tulip trees, searching out the last sweet nectar.

On *Margot* the winters were short and bitter—the days bright and dry, nights sharp and chilly. Night mists rubbed against the sides of the house, lay low under trees, coiled round the shapes of cattle as they ripped up grass with razor tongues.

I was lying next to Sherrie in the big bed. Since Tom left, we'd begun to sleep together. Sherrie was too scared to sleep alone, she was sure there were ghosts that crept from dark corners and roamed through the house in the night.

This was Tom and Sherrie's room. The room that had bulged with their secrets, their arguments. Arguments that unravelled all night long. This was the rumpled, pock-marked bed I'd often peeked at through their half-open door.

In the moonlight, the room's heavy furniture was softened and transformed; the oval mirror of the dressing table seemed to waver and swim in mid-air. We too, had changed.

I felt protective of my sister, as though I was the older, more mature one now. Sherrie had come to rely on me, instead of the other way around.

I bent over Sherrie and combed her hair with my fingers, gently and rhythmically, brushing it back from her forehead and smoothing it behind her ears. I felt her eyelashes tickle my wrist as my hand moved over her head.

I leaned back and regarded her. 'You look like a boy now, a very good-looking one.'

Sherrie giggled, and shifted in the bed. In the moonlight, her teeth were very white. Then she stopped smiling and rolled onto her back.

'Do you ever think about our father?' she whispered.

I was startled—I hadn't expected her to mention Dad. 'Yeah, a lot.' I lied.

'I think about him all the time,' she said. 'I wonder where he is, what he's doing, if he misses us. I even remember the smell of him. Cigarettes and old sweat.'

I tried not to wrinkle my nose at the smell, but all the same, I could feel it drifting around us, hanging in the air between us. I wished I could share this with her, this love of our father, but in truth, I hardly remembered him. He had left when I was four years old.

'When he was gone,' she went on, 'I felt like we were set adrift. The world was so big and scary, and there was no-one there to protect us.'

I remembered the long afternoons, when Sherrie was off at school, our mother crying aloud, her head down on the laminex table. I tried to comfort her, pet her arm as though she was a cat. Nothing helped. She'd push me away, gulp the tears down, go back to stand at the stove and sink where I could not see her face. Before long, she went back to work, weekends as well. It was Sherrie who brought me up. We moved around a lot, from country town to country town.

Sherrie was silent. I wasn't sure what to say to her.

Then a picture of Sherrie as a mean teenager flashed before me—her freckled scowl, cold blue eyes, cruel mouth. Hands pinching and pushing, and her shriek, 'No-one wants you— parasite.'

I pushed the image away and looked at Sherrie, a small hump in the bed.

Sherrie sat up and fumbled for the packet of cigarettes on the bedside table. She lit up, and for a brief moment I saw her face—her freckled cheeks tear-stained in the flare of match-light. She got out of bed, and plumped down on her pink fluffy stool at the dressing table. Her negligee shone in the moonlit room. The red tip of her glowing cigarette floated. Sherrie blew out smoke and searched around on the dressing table for somewhere to stub out her butt.

Sherrie's room had French doors leading to part of the verandah. She pushed them open and stepped outside. I followed her. We stood side by side leaning out on the verandah rail. I pressed my fingers into its rough, paint-peeling wood. She lit another cigarette. 'Dad wrote,' she said, 'three or four times. I answered at first. Then I just stopped, I don't know why.'

'Did you keep his letters?'

'No, I felt mad at him one day. I threw them in the incinerator. We lost touch.' She stabbed the words out, angry now.

I reached out to her and touched the back of her hand.

The tulip trees shivered in the slight breeze. Beyond them, out in the paddock, a beast gave a long and drawn-out moan.

Sherrie squeezed my shoulder. I could see in the moonlight she was smiling, and at the same time wiping away tears. Sherrie often smiled or laughed when she was upset. I felt the breeze off the plain, cool on my face, lifting my hair.

'Sherrie, you used to say Dad left because of me. Because I was a brat.'

'Don't be nuts.' she said. 'Sisters say things like that when they fight—you know that.'

'Tom...' I began, but snapped my mouth shut, for there was a strange and sudden sound—someone calling out in the night. We glanced at each other, startled. The voice was faint at first, and muffled, as though carried on the wind from a long way off. Then it sounded again—louder this time. A woman's high voice—the only word I could make out was 'Jesus'—but it was part of a long speech.

The voice was coming from our own paddocks. 'I think it's those people,' I whispered. 'The family.' I grasped Sherrie's hand.

The family had turned up at the house in a big yellow bus covered in peeling daisy stickers and asked Sherrie if they could stay on the land. We'd thought they meant a few days, but weeks later they were still there, camped out amongst the paperbarks, alongside our old stockyards. It was a good camping site—they had access to the road and yet were screened from view by the trees. They were rag-tag people, with wind-blown hair and faded clothes. They were brown with dust and sun, they smelt of sweat overlaid with patchouli. Their raucous children rampaged through the scrub like feral calves. They aren't a real family, Sherrie had said, they only call themselves that.

Sherrie thought they were hippies—Tom would not have approved. But Tom wasn't around anymore to make decisions. Sherrie had welcomed them onto the land, she'd accepted their screwed-up, grubby money.

The voice started again: I felt the hairs standing up on the backs of my legs. I pulled at Sherrie, 'Let's go in.'

Sherrie wouldn't budge. She was leaning out, straining to listen. 'When you go into the darkness,' called the voice, 'you may find your one true God. When you come through the blackness, you may find your most precious thing.' The voice fell away, and a sea of murmurings followed it. The wind dropped, the bush fell silent. We remained standing, still and solitary, dewy statues in the moonlight.

Until Sherrie murmured, 'Those religious nuts having a meeting. Probably harmless.' Sherrie had told me the family was religious when she'd returned from one of her visits. She didn't say much more. She was vague for the rest of the day, in her own thoughts. If I asked questions she would just shrug or turn away. She stayed closed-lipped about the family.

The silence was broken by a sudden, wild chittering. We both jumped. A flock of flying foxes crawled through the tulip trees. Moonlight gleamed on their rubbery, folded wings.

Sherrie needed to go to the loo. We held hands as we waded across the yard, through pools of darkness and pools of pearl. Her small hand was hot and moist. I waited while she sat with the dunny door open, and turned away from her hard tinkling. I remembered a black night when I'd staggered blindly across the yard and collided with a cow.

In bed I listened to her breathing change to the rhythmic whistling of sleep. I thought about Dad. I didn't know Dad—and yet, there were some memories. A few memories I'd visited and re-visited. A lap—quite bony—and a chest in a white shirt. I had stood on the lap and peeked in his ear. I could grasp the ear, but not his hair, which was short and oily. He played dinky cars with me, just like a kid, in the sandpit of some cousins. Growling the cars through furrows of damp sand.

One time I found a black eye-patch in a drawer, and held it up to mum. Mum said Dad had worn it, for months, after I'd poked him in the eye as a baby.

The sound of Sherrie's breathing filled the room. I couldn't sleep. My thoughts tumbled one after another as I lay watching the shadows of foliage tremble on the bedroom wall.

Tom had left Sherrie. He'd driven off to work one day, months ago, and we hadn't seen him since. Sherrie talked to the police, gabbled to them between her sobs. They'd stared at her, expressionless, their ruddy, fat faces a solid wall that gave nothing away. 'It happens love,' they'd told her. They reckoned he'd taken off for awhile and would probably be back. But he hadn't come back. Tom's aunts had tried to comfort Sherrie over home-made cake and sweet tea. 'It got too much,' they'd said to her, 'trying to work this barren land—and driving out to a job as well.' Sherrie didn't trust them—she thought they knew where he was, or they were hiding him. She was sad one minute, then raging. It was only lately she'd begun to settle down—since the family arrived. She was firm about staying on. 'We're not leaving, Nat,' she'd said to me, rubbing a cloth along a dusty windowsill. 'This is my place too.'

Dad left us when we were small. Mum had to work. Us girls spent a lot of time in those service station kitchens, eating our children's meals on our own, while the customers queued in a silent crowd before the counter. Mum's hands had smelt of money, onions and raw meat.

When I was older I spent weekends with the families of my friends. I was the ring-in. A part of it all, yet not really.

My friends' parents looked down benignly on our play, their hands delivered food, drinks, their brisk legs took them away to other tasks.

Unable to sleep, I had to get up and move around. I was curious about the voices, had to know what the family were up to. What was it that Sherrie saw in them? Were they her friends? Even though she acted disdainful of the family, she would disappear and visit for hours. I wasn't invited. I got the idea she was enjoying defying Tom, she'd been that mad at him. I got out of bed, fumbled into my dressing gown, felt my way through the dark house. Banjo the kelpie was on the landing outside the kitchen, sleeping as usual against the fly screen door. When he saw me he scrambled up in a great clattering of toenails, grinning and pacing in surprise.

I crossed the houseyard and headed up the path to the dam. For the first time in his life, Banjo came with me, trotting out ahead, his fox tail lifted high. I wasn't afraid of going out in the dark, but was glad to have him. It was a night like this that Sherrie had danced across the paddocks in her wedding dress, shortly after Tom had abandoned us. She'd flitted across the paddocks like a silvery ghost, twirling in and out of the trees, before collapsing and lying like a stone until dawn.

I looked back at the house, hunched dark and secluded beneath the swathe of stars. I was sure that Tom left because of me. I'd tried to tell Sherrie lots of times, what Tom had done the night of the cow, but I didn't know how to say it. The secret reminded me of those cane toads in their underground caverns, lying quiet and still in the sweltering day. You could see them through slits in the eroded land—a crowd of shining eyes.

The moon was riding bright and high, I could see nearly as well as day. The bush held hints of colour; the blurry shadows of trees streamed across the ground. On either side of the cow path, the dry winter grass stood as tall as wheat. I walked carefully, knowing that snakes were about, hunting, unseen in the tussocks.

The wind was stronger and came in gusts, tossing the heads of the trees. Trees whipped and fell, sprang back, and mingled together. They were dancing silhouettes against the sky, pointing the way to our neighbours. Something tall and black lurched away from the side of the track, and Banjo silently gave chase, his feathery backside disappearing into the scrub, so much for his company.

The voices chanted on the wind; a murmuring of many voices, faint at first, louder, then they ceased abruptly. I stood in my tracks, frozen. Nearby the cow silhouettes were clustered in the grass, their shining horns lengthening to pointed tips. The path across the paddock seemed much longer than usual. I felt I'd been plodding forever, along this narrow parting in the shivering grasses. The landscape was frosted with moon. The hills behind the farm seemed to have crowded closer, were higher, and more forbidding. They had become the lolling, untidy limbs of a giant, groaning in sleep, trees sprouting out of granite nostrils.

I reached the dam, that sullen, liquid eye. I walked along its rim, strident frog-song throbbing in my ears. As I entered the paperbark forest, a loud human chanting started up. The voices seemed to be all around me, and yet it was difficult to know exactly where they were coming from.

I stalked through the luminescent, raggedy trees, until at last I glimpsed the flickering of firelight and the dark shapes of humans. I edged closer. There was a crowd of about twenty to thirty people and I stepped in behind them.

*

Woodfires lit the clearing and sparks flew into the heads of the trees. The crowd was intent on something out front—a tall figure in black, whose face shone in the firelight. It was a woman. She stood high on a platform, a makeshift stage, and around her, facing the audience, I recognised members of the family. A bearded man strummed a guitar and sang and the audience clapped in time.

I stood behind the broad, check-shirted back of a man whose spine flexed as he loudly clapped to the music and hopped from foot to foot. His shoulder-length hair flopped rhythmically under a battered hat. There were mums holding the hands of small, sleepy children, who were rugged-up in flannelette pyjamas and dressing gowns. These were farm people, locals, and people from the town—all of us transformed in the lunar glow.

The clapping became louder, the music faster, bodies more agitated. I felt dizzy myself, and peeked out at the woman on the stage, who stood still and solitary above the confusion. The man in front of me raised his arms and jigged in a small circle. 'Jesus, Jesus,' he intoned in a strangled voice. People all around me were jerking like puppets. Out of grotesque, distorted mouths came streams of unknown words. A strange disharmony rose in the clearing. Giant shadows bounced and stretched in a savage dance.

Then, shaking arms dropped languidly and hung loose; mothers sank to the ground and nuzzled their children to their breasts; big men who were hopping and jumping hunkered down in the dust and shadows. I sat, ducking behind the check-shirted man.

The woman on the stage shouted, pointing at the audience. 'The Holy Spirit is here with us, people.' There were scattered shouts and hallelujahs from the crowd. She paused, stood silent for long minutes. A reverent quiet fell. The sounds were of crackling fire and frog-song. The tall figure on the stage lifted her arms to the sky, her face a white mask in the lunar glow.

The quiet was broken by her screech, 'There is evil amongst us, people. Look to your neighbour. Do you know him?' People were turning their heads, craning their necks. A man leapt toward me and grabbed my arm, jerking me up. I was pulled through the crowd, past pale faces that floated in shadows, past black-hole eyes boring into me. Brushing past coat-sleeves, stumbling over the log-legs of those who'd sunk down.

I was brought before the woman, who peered down at me. The man who held my arm released his grip and stepped back.

'Come up here to me,' called the woman in a soft, lilting voice. I saw fruit-box stairs at the edge of the platform, and I stumbled up them. I edged up to her, until she was so close I could feel her breath on me. Her strong scent enveloped me. Tobacco mixed with sweat.

She leaned toward me, staring with her blue, blind-looking eyes. Then she laid her hands lightly on my chest and I was thrown backwards as though by a violent push. I fell off the stage and into the cradle arms of strangers.

One of them, a woman, whispered in my ear. 'You're saved now. You're one of us.'

The bearded man strummed a chord and the crowd broke into a raucous hymn. The man and woman who had caught me when I fell still held me. I felt limp, heavy, weighed—

down, but struggled out of their arms. They did not attempt to stop me and I staggered through the crowd, tripping over legs and arms. I lingered amongst the trees on the periphery of the clearing, leaning against them. Feeling soft paperbark against my cheek and under my palms.

I watched as people lined up and took turns to approach the stage. The woman seemed to touch them lightly on the forehead or the chest, and some would fall backwards, caught by her followers, the other family members, who stood below the stage. When a person fell, I felt it too, a kind of pressure of air, that reached me, even on the periphery of the crowd. I watched the scene from my hiding place in the trees—it seemed unreal, like a play.

Before long, people began to disperse. Over-tired children were whinging, there was muted laughter and see-ya-laters. Engines revved and headlights beamed up the road.

I walked back up the track through the silver paddocks, in a trance. They had said I was one of them now. Did that mean I would go to them whenever I heard their voices? Stumble over to their camp like a sleepwalker and join them in their rituals? I still felt their strong arms holding me, and I needed to be held. I'd felt that woman's power, her touch that had sent me reeling backwards.

Though, the family scared me. I'd seen them in their make-shift camp, the dust clinging to them, the wind worrying their tangled hair, flies settling on their backs. In the late afternoons, the cries of their grubby-cheeked children would drift over from the dam. I'd spied on them, watched them washing, knee-deep in silt, the yellow water dribbling down their sun-burnt faces. They were like big families I'd known, there were too many reaching hands, too many voices, loud and rough. I was quiet, liked to be on my own. Yet, what would it feel like—to be part of such strong loyalty?

Banjo greeted me at the top of the stairs, gazing up with soft eyes. I was hungry. I lit a candle in the kitchen and searched for food. In the pantry I found some tuna which I ate straight from the tin, shovelling in the oily flesh. Banjo scratched at the fly screen, excited by the smell. When I finished I placed the tuna tin with its oil out on the landing for the dog to lick. He shoved the tin across the landing, making a loud scraping sound. Everything felt more normal.

The yard was so bright with moonlight, the elongated limbs of the jacaranda cast shadows across the silvery ground. Beyond it, the gazebo that Tom had built Sherrie out of pine off-cuts looked almost majestic. Its lines seemed straighter and taller; it glowed with a lustre it did not possess by day. But the gazebo was falling apart, made as it was out of cheap bits of timber that Tom had never gotten around to oiling.

The whole property was deteriorating. In that burst of rain we'd had, leaks pinged all night into the pots and pans we'd placed around the house. I wondered what would be left of *Margot* in years to come. The house would rot into the ground, termites chewing out the insides, until it folded in on itself. Nothing left of Tom's ancestors except their bones, turning to powder and mixing with earth. And me and Sherrie. Would there be anything left of us here? Tom's gazebo was a transitory thing, just like his love.

I climbed back into bed beside Sherrie, who was snoring like a purring cat. She was my sister. Her face was blunt, softened, carved by sleep. She looked like a child—smaller, younger than me. I twitched the blanket up to cover her bare shoulders. I put my arm around her, my hand against her ribs—where I could feel the pulse of blood.

THE FOOL

It was hard to tell where the faraway sound came from. He would hear it late at night, the soft, distant, whisper of the train. He'd never seen the train, didn't know where the tracks ran. Train must run through the thick bush behind the house-paddock. The rough bush, all gullies, rocks, fallen trees, knots of lantana.

The bush where the dogs hunted. The far-off yapping when they flushed something out. You called and called and the dogs ignored you. The dogs gone all day. They slow-trotted back at dusk across the paddocks, panting. Tongues huge and quaking, the dogs walked in slow circles, too hot to lie down.

The train raised a feeling in him, a kind of excitement. He used to imagine being inside the train, the only one awake; staring out at blackness, and his own reflection, and his own house would be just a light somewhere between the trees.

The train is heading south, through cane-fields.

Shane is trying to stay asleep, eyes screwed shut, head on his coat, coat stuffed between the seat and the window. But the carriage is brilliant with yellow light and a recorded voice announces breakfast in the dining car. Heads are up above the backs of the seats. Coughing sounds, yawns, whispers. Shane stares out at a dawn sky that's like dirty cotton wool.

In the crowded dining car he sits slumped on a high stool at the counter, paddocks—houses—cattle—fences, whizzing behind the waitresses like fake scenery unfolding in a film. His hair is greasy and hangs in his face. He hopes the hair hides the pimples that scream from his skin. His coffee rocks in his cup. Elbows nudge either side of him. He keeps his head down when the eggs are slid in front of him. 'Put that out, sir.' He looks up at the voice. 'No smoking in here, sir.' Young, unsmiling waitress, pale from the early shift.

'Who's smokin'?' The man next to Shane squashes his butt into his saucer. The girl frowns harder and swings away from the bloke's grinning horse-teeth. He's a thin-haired bloke with a rough chin, an old soft denim shirt undone to the waist. 'Well, what do ya bloody reckon about that?' The bloke jerks a thumb at the waitress and turns to Shane. His small eyes are the colour of his faded shirt. 'Ya gotta stand in the bloody corridor every time ya wanna smoke. You smoke boy?'

Shane slides his eyes away, back to the eggs that stare up, quivering on the counter. He shakes his head, 'Nah.' Hides in his shower of hair.

'Roy's the name.' He roars out his name with pleasure and offers a hand, nicotine yellow. Roy's handshake is jerky and rapid. He leans on the counter, like it's a bar-room. Goes to pull out his smokes from his top shirt pocket, remembers, clicks his fingers in mid-air. Shane notes the gold earring, the white scar at his throat. Who is this guy? Gypsy? Wanderer? Poofta?

'Where you headin' for kid, the big smoke? Sydney?'

Shane nods into his eggs, looks out past the waitresses to the sugar cane and the strip of sky. It'll be cane, cane, cane, for a long way to come, with a little wooden house on stilts tucked into it here and there, a woman and a kid on the front verandah, waving at the train.

The train bumps Roy against him, the smoky voice saws on, 'I've been around mate, been everywhere man, as the song goes. Been to Cairns, been to Tassie. Originally from Engadine. I've lived in Sydney. Newtown, Surry Hills, Erko, Chippo. The Cross. Now there's a place for ya. Ohhhoo, I tell ya. That strip of street at night with them buskers and fortune-tellers. Them bruiskers outside the strip joints, herdin' them in. The pro's. Them girls in their little minis an' fish-net stockings. Ahh. But you wouldn't go in for that sort of thing, would ya boy? Don't smoke. Bet you don't drink. Bet you're a virgin and all.' Roy elbows him in the shoulder.

The boy flushes red and snorts, looks around to see if anyone else heard.

'Hey boy, I know just the one for you.' Roy puts his face close to the boy's ear. 'She's nearing six-foot in her stilettos. Old as your mum, I'll bet.' Roy draws back, chortling. 'Yay, Rosie,' he whispers into his coffee. 'You want me to keep talking, boy?'

Shane half-smiles and shrugs, he's not sure.

'Then buy me a drink, boy.' Roy slaps his big hand on the counter. 'Waitress.'

'We don't serve alcohol 'til ten,' the waitress says.

'Oh fuck, c'mon, let's get outta here. I gotta little something in me coat pocket.' Roy slides off his stool and the boy follows, edging through the crowded car past families, kids crushed round tables laughing at sliding sauce bottles.

Roy prowls through the corridor in his faded denim, cowboy belt buckle flashing. Shane's strides are long and light, he's nimble in the jerking train. His flannelette shirt is loose on his thin, rounded shoulders. His face masked by his hair. Outside the Men's they loiter, leaning into the vibrating carriage walls. Roy gulps from a bottle of whisky and passes it to Shane. The boy swigs at the bottle, feeling the warmth start in the muscles of his legs. They stare out the window at the blur of trees, the fast-running telephone wires.

Shane squats down on the rollicking floor. Far away now. The old man must be real mad. His dad like a cloud of blow-flies, stamping and swearing and throwing things around. He shuts out the image of his red-faced father. This is the train. When he was a little kid, he used to listen for the sound of its distant clashing, used to try to get a glimpse of it from the ridge behind the house. But he never saw the train. He'd thought that maybe there was no train. No-one else ever heard it, at least they never said.

From up on the ridge you could see all over—the dirt roads scribbling through the scrub, half a hill planted up with ragged, shiny banana trees, flat square paddocks of cane, so green it hurt your eyes. In the distance were the hills, woolly with scrub, and the mountain they called The Big Nipple, because it looked like a proud, high tit, poking at the sky. You couldn't see the town, only a few houses of fibro or bessa. Sandra's place, down on the flat. His place, up from the dam. The dam staring up. A yellow eye. All summer the kids played there, slinging mud and the floating cowshit, swimming and diving, wrestling in the clay-coloured water.

Summers went on and on, like the sky, like the drought. Waiting. Getting bored and waiting for school to start. Then leaving school and waiting to get on the dole.

Last summer he'd spotted Sandra Marello strutting around in the scrub with her shirt up, swinging a skinny doll. She caught sight of him, floating neck-deep in the dam and she quickly slid her t-shirt back over her nipples, and he pretended he hadn't seen.

She made her way over to the dam bank and squatted by his clothes. They stared at each other. 'Coming in?' he'd invited, but she shook her head and looked away. He bobbed closer, flicking teasing sprinkles of water, spitting water in thin jets through the gap in his front teeth. He could see the bumps of her nipples through her t-shirt. He'd thought how he'd seen her lately, running, holding her breasts in the palms of her hands. He shot his fist through the water, soaking her, and she scrambled up and retreated. He laughed.

'Piss off moron,' she yelled. She picked up a rock and threw it near his head. 'Piss off yasself you slut,' he'd screeched out. 'Go on. Go home.'

She found another rock and hurled it across the water, just missing him. The cicadas' rhythm could be heard up the hill. Under the gums with their hard, still leaves. At the yards, with their memories of blood and branding and cattle-dip.

She'd grabbed his clothes from the bank and ran up the hill with them toward the house. He squirms, remembering how she'd lined up her little brothers and sisters to watch him come back from the dam. He had to march up the paddock in only his thongs, his hands on his crotch, pretending not to care. Ignoring the kids chucking rocks at him from the cover of the lantana. He'd stamped towards them when they came near, and the girls would fling away, screaming.

'Joe Blake.' He got her back with that. He'd scared the shit out of her, making out he'd seen a snake when they were mucking around out in the paddocks. But after a while she got wise to him and took no notice. His face reddens at the memory of it, how pathetic he was.

The train is twisting through low country of canefields and sinuous, bulging rivers. Roy tips his bottle and gulps. 'You in love? That what you running away from, boy?' Shane shrugs, looks away from the crazy man to the flashing cane and the sky.

'You know, boy, this here train is a love train. You're on it, an' it's going in a circle, around and around—whoooo-wheee. An' we're all fools for love, boy, don't you know?'

A pregnant woman stumbles through the corridor and Roy tucks the bottle quickly into his coat.

'What are you talking about?' mumbles Shane. When the woman's gone, Roy hands him the bottle. Shane passes it back.

'Too early.'

'What's that, boy?'

'Too early for me, man.'

Roy sucks on his rollie, lets the smoke slide slowly out his mouth and nostrils. 'This train, she's a love train. I'm sure.'

Roy rubs the sandpaper of his face, raises the bottle and sucks again. The burning liquid bubbles at his lips. He licks his teeth, squinting out the carriage window. He frowns back at Shane.

'Can you imagine, boy, being trapped in one of them cane-cutter's huts with a fat, slab-footed woman and a muster of slimy-faced, pot-bellied brats? Pickin' tomatoes in the summer. There's no life in that, boy. I give it all away.'

Shane remembers certain plots of earth, the dry, grey dirt. Tomatoes in boxes on the front veranda. A couple of flies, dainty, tasting at the green, shiny skins. He felt like gathering himself up, swinging out the clanking door and flying into the cooling cane. Rest in the depths of it there like a raggedy insect. Burrow down its green rustling to where the earth begins, and stay put.

'Cicada's wing.' Shane holds it up. A strong, green-veined, crackling thing. He smooths the wing segments with the tip of his finger.

'Hey boy,' Roy says, irritated. 'If you hear them ticket-collectors come a marchin' give us a hoy. I ain't got a ticket.'

After dark, the passengers form into garrulous groups, hunched over endless card-games, life-story swapping, beer-swilling. Roy's at the centre of it all, gesticulating, roaring, slapping down cards, getting drunker and drunker.

The train is running faster, careering, roller coasting. Shane thinks the corridor is like the fun-house at a show; the floor fevered, shuddering, doors between carriages swinging and slamming. At three am Shane finds Roy collapsed in the corridor. No-one else awake. He drags the man through the dark carriage, brushing past stuck-out legs, elbows, heads. Shane's own seat is the only one he can put him in.

Back in the corridor the boy lingers by the cold water fountain. Empty juice bottles roll around his feet. The thou-sand creaks and squeaks of the train. Outside, there is only blackness, stars, unknown hills, mountains, paddocks. They pass through land speckled with fire. Bushfires? Burning off?

'I'm ready.' He'd turned up his face, and she advanced on him, holding up the perfume-smelling thing.

'Lay back and shut your eyes.' She sat cross-legged on the lavender quilt, leaning over him, examining his face, holding up the eye-shadow set, with its paint-box colours, its Imperial Purple, Meadow Pink, Victorian Blue. The room was dim, the bed high and hard. He closed his eyes and the feathery light brushes began, tickling his lids. He didn't move until she gave him the hand-mirror, and then he sat up, winking one eye and then the other, his lids heavy under eye-shadow the colour of bruises. She gently pushed him back and slid a mascara stick under his lashes, combing the thick stuff into them until they stood stiff and black.

She powdered his face, tapping and rubbing until his fat brown freckles had disappeared. She smoothed on the red-brown lipstick, making his thin lips fuller, wider, wet-looking. He was Aladdin Sane, he was Ziggy Stardust. In the half-lit room, he was the prettiest star. He held the hand-mirror for her while she did her own eyes, rubbing on thick green shadow out of a tube. While she scrutinised her face, Shane watched their two reflections in the mirror.

In the train's windows, Shane's face is superimposed on the dark landscape, his reflection wavers, ghost-like. Sandra shot off her big mouth about those make-up sessions in her mum's bedroom. How old was he then? Twelve or thirteen and she was about ten. Her brothers were tough boys, yobbos, hung around in a group of yobbos.

The boys saunter up the street, all walking as if something's stuck up their arse. Shirtless, beige torsos smudged with blue-green tatts, arms slow-swinging, fist around a can. Thongs flap. Jeans hang down, showing arse cracks. That bloke with cobwebs tattooed on his elbows and fat Ernie Hart with his slug-like back, torpedo head and ready fists.

Passing, you look down. Don't dare catch their eye. Faces surround you and close in. The arms swing out, fingers ready to grasp. Tough boys, treading heavy and slow through the town, all walking as if something's stuck up their arse.

That time he got surrounded over at Marello's place by Sandra's brothers. They were out in the scrub, the dolly-bush up to his chest. They were all around him, their shirts off, torsos glistening. He flung himself forward to break through the circle, but one of them, the biggest brother with the flabby stomach, leapt to head him off. Like he was a young bull in a yard, about to be castrated.

He tried to run fast, but it felt like slow-motion. Scrambling and pushing his way through the bush, through dolly bush and prickly ti-tree, over fallen logs. It was as though the bush had trapped him, hugging him to itself. They caught him and swung him up, writhing. He saw their hairy calves as they carried him and the crackling bush clawed at his face. They held him down and pulled off his shorts. One of them shook a knife in his face. He lay very still, whimpering. A fist grabbed his penis and he grew under the swift wanking. Then they smeared boot polish over his dick and balls. The caustic stuff ate him—he roared out his anger and pain until he almost frightened them. When they released him, he kicked one of them hard in the balls, not caring about the consequences; he'd thought they couldn't hurt him worse than this.

The train is slowing. It strains and coils above valleys. He looks down on mists smearing the roofs of farms. The light has come, colour is oozing into things. Dairy country. White rocks leap from velvet paddocks. Through holes in mist he glimpses enormous Angus cows strolling toward their morning milking. He thinks of knobs of mushrooms in the wet grass fed on pools of cowshit. Pancakes of shit baking in the sun.

Roy is gone from his seat so Shane flops down and dozes, despite the hot dazzlement of the lights and the stampeding of restless children up and down the aisle.

The train jerks into some country town. Railway workers, trackside, wave them in. Over the platform, hanging baskets of ferns. In the green shade a small huddle of people hug and kiss and say goodbye.

Leaving. The morning Shane left he'd been lucky. The man in the ticket office at the station in town didn't know him. The only other person on the platform was an Aboriginal lady with a stroller and a toddler on her hip. She didn't know him either.

He'd taken the money. That'd been easy, too. He knew its hiding place on the top of the cupboard. His dad was old-fashioned—he never believed much in banks. Shane remembers flipping through the bills in the dark kitchen, deciding not to take all the money. The wad of notes he shoved in his pocket seemed like enough.

He left when his dad was down at the pub, his sister away, no-one else home. He'd been planning it for years. It was three months after his sixteenth birthday. He left after dark, slept at the showgrounds, by the creek with its ribs of scum and fringe of bobbing rubbish. Woke up at dawn to catch the train.

His dad would kill him. His dad the local farrier. After mum died, he became the local ladies' man. He shod all the pony club horses of the young girls in the town. The girls would stand holding the reins, watching the big man bent over, the hair growing off his shoulders. The big man in shorts and work-boots, his strong sweat smell. The ponies leaned right on him as he worked on them, holding a hoof between his thighs. It fucked up his back. He'd wanted Shane to take over one day but the boy never took to it; riding, the farm, doing physical things. 'You're soft, boy.' He'd heard it all his childhood.

That time the old man put him on a pony, and it took off. He was eight, or nine, jogged up the paddock, his hands clutched the pommel when the old man wasn't looking. He almost enjoyed the feeling of the pony moving under him. Circled the pines, glimpsed bright brown needles, broken mushrooms, toadstools; felt the feathery lower pine branches as they brushed his shoulder. On the way back, the pony started galloping, heading for the gate, galloping straight past his dad, who was yelling, 'Lean back, pull him up.' But he lost the reins and there was nothing but the sound of hoofs and a loud screaming. Then the fall. Couldn't breathe, tight to bursting, all the air knocked out of him. Lying there, rolling on the ground, holding onto his stomach, he thought he was going to die.

His dad was standing over him. 'C'mon, yer only winded. Gotta get back on that horse if we can catch the bastard or you'll lose your nerve.'

'No. I'm sick,' he whimpered. He kept on lying there, watching the billions of beautiful twirling silver fish, somer-saulting over the red face of his father, and the blue strip of sky beyond.

'You was screaming like a girl,' sneered the old man.

The horse shifted in the distance, trailing its reins. It blew through its nose, a disdainful sound. He lost his nerve all right. Never got on again after that.

The train is still stalled at the station, some town or suburb he doesn't know, has never heard of. Shane stares out at the meld of people. The old man developed a contempt for him. He criticised everything Shane did, he was impossible to please. In the end it seemed better to be a bastard and take his cash.

Thinking of the money, Shane checks the pockets of his coat—and nothing's there. The money's gone. Shit, fuck, shit. He grabs and grabs at the empty coat. Pokes between the hard cushions of his seat, scrabbles around on the floor. In the seats in front of him are two elderly ladies and across from them a Down Syndrome girl in her twenties who is nursing a black baby doll. The old women are chattering, in whispers and whistles, their nodding heads shiny and soft above the seats. He wants to tap their shoulders and ask if they've seen anyone meddling with his coat—but how can he? He doesn't want people asking questions, can't risk drawing attention to himself. He charges through the train, searches every carriage, every Men's toilet. Roy. It has to be. Old bastard.

Back in his seat he stares out. The bristling tiled roofs of new housing estates spin away from the train. The outer suburbs of a big city. He could hop on the next train home— if he had the fare. He could turn himself in at the cop-shop. He arches up to feel inside the stiff pockets of his jeans. Ten dollar note, wrapped around a bit of change. Might be a bit of coin in his bag. And Sandra had told him the Hare Krishnas give you a free feed. That money, he never even counted it.

The city can be felt a long way off. The city waits. The magnified generator hum of its centre. The back-beat is the click of high-heels on the tiled floors of malls. Out on the harbour, ferries slide about like molluscs. The train rolls into Central and the boy steps off onto concrete.

AT THE FENCE

There she is, walking at the side of the empty highway; the greenie girl with the big pack that bends her over. He pulls up but she keeps on walking, trying to ignore the sleazy-slow car and the man gesturing, offering a lift.

The girl keeps up her pace, looking straight ahead. Feels the breath of the car at her heel. Ahead of her the mirage of the town shivers inside the haze. The girl crosses the road and the man in the dirty white Holden shrugs his shoulders and accelerates.

She is walking over a flat plain of red stones, beneath a blue denim sky. She is the only thing moving in this world. Last night, after the coach had dropped her, she'd wandered a little way into the plain, fell asleep on the ground under some bushes, and was startled awake by the bright rhythmic flashing of an endless train, carriages of cars piled upon cars, silhouettes of men standing in open boxcars. After the assault of the train, the silence returned, and she had lain watching the lightening sky. She gathered up her things when she thought it was late enough and walked back to where the coach had dropped her, to the roadhouse, where the louvres were shut tight against the dust, and on the door was a scrap of cardboard with, *no greenies allowed* scrawled in red ink.

She pushed open the door and entered, and he had watched her get ordered out again. He was on a stool at a bar, sipping his morning stubby. The room had fallen silent, the locals turned to her with hard faces. 'Didn't you see the sign?' the blond waitress had snarled. 'You aren't welcome here.'

She was shaken. She thought she would walk to the town then, and ring up the organisers from there—they could radio for someone to pick her up.

She hadn't realised how far it would be. She can see Woomera lying ahead of her in a blaze of tin roofs, but she doesn't seem to be getting any closer. The town might be receding as she tramps toward it.

When the car returns, she thinks, shit, this is it-he's brought his mates. But he's alone. He crackles out in his ocker accent, 'Come on slow coach, hop in. I'm going out to the mine, I'll drop you with your friends.' His red face beams through the car window.

She peers back at him. What can she do? She hauls open the heavy door and gets in the back.

'Hey I'm harmless. I'm only worried about yer,' he says.

He waves cigarettes at her. She has rollies. She rolls a dry and skinny smoke. He chats. When he addresses her he adjusts the rear-vision mirror so he can look at her, and she can see his face. He's in his forties or fifties, she thinks. Not young. He has tufts of black hair in his nostrils. He drives with one hand slack on the wheel. She sees that the hand is red and square and the nails grey and bitten down.

They drive through Woomera, which is modern and ugly. She's read about it. A purpose-built place, set up at the end of

World War Two for British weapons-testing. Until last year it was off limits to everyone except defence personnel. The man drives through flat and vacant streets and she goggles out the window at the small suburban houses. Near the town begins the prohibited area, an enormous chunk of desert, that's used for rocket launches, weapons testing, spacecraft tracking. Maralinga was part of it—an atomic testing site, where atom bombs were set off in the fifties and the desert-dwelling Aboriginal people, who weren't warned about the bombing, were contaminated by radiation. A lot of it has been de-restricted, but it still takes up an area of one hundred and twenty-seven square kilometres—she knows the information by heart: it's the largest landlocked testing range in the world.

They are through the town and out again. The road becomes dirt, the country red and yellow. The man remembers the stubby in the glove-box. He cracks it open and gurgles it down. The beer is warm but he needs to drink—he's always thirsty. He's a man from a country of rivers.

'Dry country,' he remarks, tilting the mirror. 'Been before?'

She says it's her first time in the desert, first time as a protester. 'They seemed to know straight away back there that I was headed out to the blockade.'

He laughs, 'It's that time of year—when the greenies come. You see them at the gates and on the tv. They're up from the cities, unemployed and students, in their special buses with slogans on the side. You don't generally see them trying to walk out to the mine, though. Most of them have more sense.'

She frowns at him but does not feel like biting at the bait. Her back aches, her throat is raw and sore, but she smokes and smokes. The man digs at her with his eyes and will not let her be.

'It's all bullshit,' he says. 'You'll never stop it, never. Those hippies out there—barefoot, rolled in red dirt. No water to wash with and they like that. They try to tell you that you will die. Bullshit. We've got blokes coming up from the city checking the radiation. You know, once I saw a greenie stake a flag on a tailings dump. Couldn't believe it. No way would miners touch that stuff, and here was this long-haired jerk…'

'You don't recognise our right to protest.'

'You've got no right to take my job.'

She turns from him, stares out the window. A hawk glides its circuit of sky. She wishes she was free of the hard and tankish car, and this man, a uranium miner, who is determined to give her an ear-bashing as he drives her across the plain of stones.

She says, 'You live out there, at the mine?'

'Yeah,' he says. 'It's home, sorta. Ten years. Demountable house. A bit of green lawn—some of the wives make gardens.' He tosses the stubby out the window. 'Once, in the old days, there was cattle out here—a homestead or two. Hard to believe, isn't it?'

They pass a mob of brumbies standing not far off, incurious, stamping at flies. 'The Blacks call this place, End of the Walkabout. That's what my mate, Chalky Tupper reckoned. He was married to a Black girl. Abos have all gone now. Else they're down at the fence with the greenies.'

'Forced off their land.' She gazes out at the land that is hard and sealed against them.

'Land's only good for what it's got under it.'

It was only the other day when he drove out he saw they were down at the fence again. Saw their tents and flags. It was that time of year. He'd gotten out of the car to go and say g'day to Chalky Tupper, but there was no Chalky. Some bloke he'd never seen the likes of before. A security guard, US military-style, in khaki shirt and trousers, had marched out of the gateshed—demanded his card, scrutinised it, and asked him to repeat his name.

'Des Norman.' He said his tough plain name, staring straight ahead. He snatched his card back. They were these new cards issued with mug shots, and even the old cheese had to have one. Anyone'ud think it was a bloody police state and all because of the dammed demonstrators camped in the sandhills.

Then the other night driving back from town they'd stopped at the greenies' camp for a perv, and besides, Pete had needed a chunder. But they'd gotten off the track somehow and into the sand. He'd headed straight for the islands of fire and faces in the dunes—he'd wanted something to happen, he was bored, sobering up.

He wouldn't have minded just squatting down at that fire and drinking his left-over stubbies and getting offered some billy tea. Hadn't sat round a fire drinking and talking since he was a young fella. But the boys wouldn't let him do that. George turned up the car cassette player full-blast. Larry was pissing behind the car, and Pete blundered off for a spew. Larry got out the carton of stubbies and plonked them on the hood—then blinding light—what the fuck? There were these two greenie sheilas with torches, big frowning sheilas they were. Two strong circles of light.

He cracked open a stubby and held it out. 'Here, love,' he said, 'have a beer.' The girls ignored his swaying, outstretched arm.

That was greenies for you, sending the women over. Fucking piss-weak, pathetic. Bastards always pushed the women forward—pooftas, cunts. Toby Black said he jobbed a greenie once and this woman jumped in between them and the greenie stood back. When the greenies faced the cops, it was the same. Screaming sheilas in the front line, men at the back, and if a woman has a trog on her hip, so much the better.

'Pooftas.' He'd called out at the group at the fire, who were standing now and talking amongst themselves.

'Cops coming, Des,' said Pete in his ear.

Pete was pulling at him, shoving him into the car, 'C'mon—let's piss off.' Maybe afraid he was going to get into a rage and start throwing punches. Like he'd done before.

The girls were looking even bolder, standing their ground, shining their torches. It was all a bit of a blur, but next minute he was behind the wheel, trying to start the car. Cops were bloody everywhere, this time of year. If he lost his license, bloody hell—the old cheese 'ud have to drive him around.

Someone was shoving something under the tyres, and the mates were out and ready to push. There were people all over the bloody car, the girls with their torches, greenies.

'Give her a go now, Des.' He pressed the accelerator, heard the wheels scrape and sand spray, the mates jumped in, doors slammed, and the car heaved out and they were off, on the track again. He'd thought he'd heard a cheer in the background.

Larry had said: 'I reckon they were all sheilas back there, the lot of them.'

'Give over, mate,' he'd laughed. 'Yer blind.'

George said, 'If they were all sheilas, and not a cop in sight, where are we bloody going?'

Pete said that when he was chucking a girl came up behind him and told him she'd rung the cops.

'Yeah,' said Larry, 'on the bloody telephone. I'll be buggered, she put one over yer.'

But they'd kept on driving, hoping they'd get through the gates okay. They were out of cigarettes, missing their wives' warm backs and the hum of the buses at shift change at the mine.

He glances in the mirror at the girl on the backseat. 'We stumbled into the leso's camp the other night. All birds, they were.' She's not a bad little sort. Pale skin and freckles. That red glow to her. If he was still young, he'd try something. Not that he was all that old. She'll get burned out here—the sun will dry her up, wrinkle her up. Not made for this country—but who is? Only the Blacks. These greenies, they make you mad, you want to hurt them. But look at her, just a nervous kid, huddled there on the backseat.

She ignores him. She's not afraid. Only a little afraid. She sees herself as a bold girl—she takes risks, she always had. She's a child of the age of big bombs. A lucky child. Born on Hiroshima Day, many years after the event. Birthdays have echoed with nuke-age jargon all her life. Hiroshima, Nagasaki, bomb bomb bomb. Atomic attack—bells, whistles, sirens, flash. Obliteration. Heat waves carbonised bodies radioactive poisoning.

When she was a little kid, her chubby hands tore at clean, new, bright pink cutsie-patterned birthday paper. She toddled in front of the big tv, bathed in its blue flicker. Crowd shots flashed, demonstrators surged, pickets waved. Newsreaders' serious mouths fast-moving.

These days the colour portable tele with the bad reception spoke from the kitchen counter in the house she shared in the city. Arms race, nuclear proliferation—vertical, horizontal and geographic, President Reagan, South Pacific, nuclear ships free zone, real peace and disarmament initiatives, arms control tests bans tests bans tests bans. She wonders if we'll get through the eighties, survive the next few years. Though the war happens so fast it doesn't ever happen.

She shoved her army pants, her japara, her boots in her pack, pulled the cord, tight. Slammed the door and caught the bus to the desert.

The uranium miner thought she was a hippie, but she was never a hippie. When she was a young kid the bare-foot women would come into town shopping, their faded wrap-around Indian skirts flapping at their ankles, their little blond babies strapped to their backs or their fronts. Skinny bearded men drove dented utes with rainbow transfers on the back windows. There were rumours of communes in the bush and dope plants caged in chicken wire. As a kid she smoked cigarettes stolen from her mother, down at the creek. One time she sat the whole afternoon with a compact mirror, watching smoke furl out her nostrils, then she spewed. It didn't stop her—now she chain-smoked.

At age fifteen she despised herself, hated her fair hair and freckles. Boys teased her, her brothers teased her. She wanted to hide herself, hide out. So she haunted the deserted local library where only a few old men sat rustling newspapers and clearing their throats, and where the red-lipsticked Queen smiled down from the wall. She leaned over books. Her glasses flashed under the fluorescents.

The lady librarian would not check out her book, slid it down under the counter. 'Too old for you, young lady. Shouldn't be on the shelf, where a child can pick it up.' She hadn't argued then—she'd looked away, embarrassed.

But deep inside her, something simmered. A river of anger bubbled there.

She'd grown up with men who wouldn't let her speak—so she learned to raise her voice. She'd raise her voice, then he'd raise his voice until the room, the street, the building, the town would be filled with the sounds of yelling. Loudmouth, they called her, when she came home with all her big ideas, her big city ideas.

She says, 'Do you think about where the stuff goes to, what it's used for, the massive build-up of nuclear arms, all over the world?'

He laughs into the mirror. 'Won't happen, love. If it did, if we die—we die, that's it. Don't know why you cranks bother.'

'What about your kids. Don't you care about your kids? Want them to have a future?'

'Yeah, I care about my kids. That's why I work, to give 'em something one day. Reckon I provide for half the hippies at the fence and all.'

They were kids from his first marriage. Probably the girl's age, the eldest. He'd only seen them in photos, since they were little ones. Two unsmiling boys in shorts, posing on the riverbank, arms folded across their bare chests. That brown river. The river that flowed by Penny and the kids, the river that he knew, that was under his eyelids. The river travelled past the house on stilts, where Penny had stood, staring out, hands in the washing-up, bare legs, bare feet on the lino, staring out at the brown fast river rising. Her brown, bare legs. The vein standing out at the back of one knee. Boys on the floor revving battered dinky cars. He was stretched out beside them, pretending to play, but his head turned toward the tv, watching the news. Banana rotted under a cloud of fruit flies on the laminex table and soon the steak would be

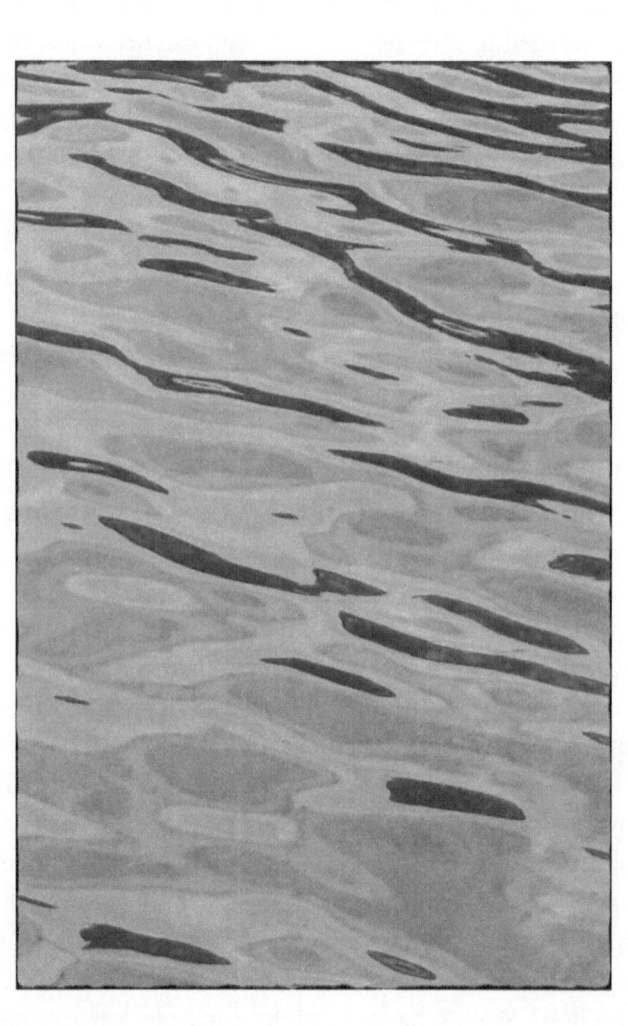

on the plates, meat juice oozing into mashed potato. And they'd be sitting round the table, Penny cutting up the steak for the boys, chinking knives on the white plates, his shirt off, torso wet with sweat. The wet heat you got up there. Chewing and talking, the boys telling every silly joke they'd heard.

At flood-times you could fish off the back verandah. Plenty of tucker. Kids cut off from school hooned up the flooded back roads in motor boats tugging groups of other kids on toboggans. The Fletchers who lived across the river in a rotting shack you could only get to by boat got their sisters pregnant and went to gaol. Women cracked up and cursed at the pouring rain that crashed on tin roofs while little kids rode tight circles on tricycles on the lino and leaks punkered into buckets and basins all night long.

Rain rain rain rain. Here, it hadn't rained at all for thirteen years. Up there in the river country the land was so low and warm and so green it hurt your eyes. Barefoot girls thumped across the sway-backed floors of those old wooden houses on stilts. Sticky little green frogs bubbled your laundry walls. Snakes slid out of fields of thick green cane and into bedrooms, insects twanged electrically all night long. You sat in open front doorways, coloured strips of grimy plastic fluttering at your back, and the kids yelling, yelling.

Those boys, his boys. Blond, cherubic-looking, but real little brats. Broke anything in five minutes. At the wedding she was five months pregnant and everyone knew but nobody cared. It was what happened.

He didn't say goodbye to the boys. Watched them for a few minutes while they slept, purring, tangled in bedsheets. Left. Left Penny to a loveless, sleepless night, stamped down the creaking wooden paint-peeling steps, and got in the ute and drove. He ended up driving trucks for years and taking up with waitresses.

But the river was always under his eyelids, flowing through his life as it had his mother's. He thought he could hear the sounds of water—but it was only his thirst; he thought he could smell the choppy river, but it was only dust. The slow flow in summer, then at flood-times the ferocious river unravelled a trail of garbage, broken branches, dead animals, and in later years tourists came by on the slow ferry, eating chicken, flapping their dead hands at you. You ignored them, looked away and went on with your fishing. He wondered if the yabbies still tinkered amongst the debris of the shallow pools, their tails blazoned in tiger-stripes. How still he'd squatted, as a boy. Had watched them move through slashes of light, the reflected trees, cautiously toward the bait, the ball of rotten meat. He remembers plunging in on steaming days, and all the things the river brought.

No river now—just the rippled peaks of the dunes where no-one walks. The dunes that are on fire. The sand that stains you red. The little clean white delicate bones.

He slows. The gibber plain has given way to softer country. She looks out at blue-grey scrub, a tender, fleshy sand. Then she catches sight of the flapping tents scattered across the dunes, a bright sweep of desert flowers. The vehicles are hung with banners and bright-painted slogans. The kombi vans in every shade of orange and ochre. An old Sydney double-decker bus is piled high with tents and camping gear. Flags—the Aboriginal flag, others painted with rainbows, bright moons and stars—burr in the desert wind. Excitement surges in her—she's travelled a long way for this.

Greenies everywhere. Groups of greenies strolling up the road. He sticks his arm out the window, he waves and nods and grins, eyes the legs of the women in shorts and thongs, kicking up the dust as they walk.

The girl on the backseat looks straight ahead or down, embarrassed at being with the man. But when at last he pulls up and lets her out she turns and takes his hand. 'I'm glad I didn't have to walk.' The heavy pack is on the ground, between them. 'See you down at the fence,' he says.

She looks around. A man on stilts, in Uncle Sam trousers, hurries along the road, cocks his top hat at her. A child runs with a yellow kite, which bumps along the ground behind. She'll look for her affinity group, who should be here, some-where, by now. Some people are squatting in the dirt, talking, so she walks that way, to find a place to go.

THE RETURN

Ellie was the eldest, the only girl. The only child who knew her dad. She'd think of how he had read to her, sitting by her bed. She could still see his face, his downcast eyes, blond lashes gentle as he sounded out the words. His face glowed reddish in the room's dim light. His big sausage fingers lingered upon the pages of the book. When he dimmed the oil lamp and left, and the moon's bare face stared into the room, she'd play in the rumpled bed as her quilts turned silver.

In the morning when she'd get out of bed and into the cold, he'd already be gone. His scent was gone, all that was left was a cloud of fried egg smell, thick in the house. Ellie's mum, Sharon, was staring out the window at the rain, her belly taut and round and hard.

It rained a lot in those days, a constant tinkering in downpipes and splattering into puddles in the yard. The bush shone with rain, the eucalypts were slick with it. Black cockatoos, cawing with joy, hung upside down in the trees. The rain would set in, it would go on for days, for weeks.

Sharon remembered ten straight days of heavy rain—a thundering on the tin roof, a sound of bullets as a sun-shot spray of hail went plinkering across the yard.

The small house shrunk even further into itself, turning its back to the rain as a horse or a cow will do. Sharon resigned herself. She settled like a sigh into the patched easy chair by the pot belly stove, and took up her knitting. Ellie, stir crazy, chased the cat, climbed over and over the couch, screaming like a banshee. It was the rain that year that got to them, that split up her and Barry, Sharon was sure of that. When she stood in mud and opened the chook pen that morning and saw all of them drowned, white dirty lumps, she screamed up at the grubby sky. She'd loved her chooks, so had Ellie. Ellie had sat in the pen and crooned with them, tried to imitate their voices. Sharon dug a pit to bury them, and it filled up with yellow water. Then Barry roused on her for being an idiot, pregnant and all, standing out digging holes in the rain.

Sharon's world was the small house, the house that Barry built out of scavenged wood and tin. Beyond their cleared block the bush fanned out, impermeable, unknowable. They were out on the edge, as they'd intended to be, living in the back-blocks, between the forest and the town, a borderland.

Sharon began to wonder, during those times of rain. If no-one sees me, maybe I don't exist? But there was Ellie, sleeping on the rug on the floor. And there was the baby rippling inside of her, its limbs stretching out, flexing. Her belly distended as though it were a sheet of rubber.

In the mad rush to hospital when she was about to have Luke, they were almost cut off. The ute strained over the causeway, the current pulling against the wheels, sliding them toward the flooded creek. 'Keep going, keep going,'

Sharon urged Barry. Ellie sat between them, stared out at yellow, rushing water—no road, only water, and only the tips of shrub and grass. Ellie was a non-stop talker, and her new brother Luke didn't utter a word until he was four. Barry was long-gone by then.

After Barry left for good, Sharon kept on having babies, as if to populate the little house full to bursting. That's what people said. Ellie and Luke were his, but Matthew, Mark and John had different fathers.

Sharon took root, she sprouted babies. She planted herself on the land—in the land. Kids' toys, tricycles, multi-coloured, flowed out of the house and into the yard. There were no real flowers, the next lot of chooks saw to that, and the tree fern she planted soon died, dried up in the sun.

No-one had expected her to stay. Women from around the district visited Sharon with their toddlers and babies-they brought gifts, pot plants, home-made jams, armfuls of silver-beet and winter apples. Sometimes the women took Sharon to the new-built ashram at Black Mountain for kiirtan, and they sat and chanted amidst the smell of pine, with the two chubby and smiling monks whose bald heads shone with reflected light. Sharon and her children fed the gift apples to the horses, the children ate the jam from the jar, pot plants withered on window-sills.

Around the perimeters of the cleared land, the bush was a dead weight. Loggers had access through Sharon's place, and in the season their massive trucks trammelled up the dirt road past the house. Sharon was afraid the kids might get run over.

In autumn, she took the kids mushroom-picking. Ellie kept the little ones out of the cow-pats while Sharon stalked ahead, scanning for the circles of small white knobs in the grass.

In winter, Sharon split wood every evening for the combustion stove, sometimes in the rain. Her tendons strained as she smacked the blockbuster down. Water froze in the pipes, splitting the pvc.

A man came to the house once a week. He was known in the district as 'Big Harry'. Three months later Sharon got her tent dresses out of moth-balls.

In summer, she took the kids down to the river, where they ran naked, paddling in the sun-split, rushing water. They filled buckets with blackberries from the bushes on the bank. Sharon couldn't think what she would do without Ellie, without the girl.

*

When Ellie next sees her dad, she's eleven. Her limbs are long and honey-brown. She no longer talks all the time. She's tall, she's as thin as a stick. Her mother calls her a *gumby*. She's not sure what that means.

Ellie and Luke and Matthew have just got off the school bus when they spot a ute, one they haven't seen before, parked up by the barn. They jog up the drive, school bags bumping. A man is jiggling a key in the barn door. His red hair shines—he's bald on top. Sharon stands outside the house, with the rifle, cradling it like a baby. The little ones are shut inside, Ellie can hear them crying. The man starts swearing, kicking at the barn door. Ellie and the boys stand and watch.

'Come here you kids, get inside,' Sharon commands.

The boys obey, Ellie ignores her. 'Who's that?' But she knows.

Ellie, tall and thin, stands gazing at the man who wrenches open the barn door and disappears inside. Her mother, poppy-eyed, screeches at her to get in the house.

Ellie walks up to the barn, looks inside. She's never seen inside before. It was a new-built barn of galvanised iron, locked up ever since he left. She steps into the dark, into the clutter, amid hulking shapes of machinery, objects shrouded by sheets, shelves of boxes, tools, ladders. And the man is there, bending over something, a crate on the floor.

Ellie says hi. The man stiffens, spins around. They stare at each other. She sees his eyes in the dim light, but she can't read them.

She runs up to him, she flings her arms around him. 'Dad.' His arms enclose her, he pats her back. But she senses something strange in the hug, something not quite right. There's resistance in the solid body of her father.

She steps back. 'Dad?'

'Ellie. You must be.' His voice is strained and soft. 'How old are you?'

'I'm twelve.'

She wants to hug him again, to draw him into herself. She wants all of him. 'Why'd you come back?'

But the man is speechless. He opens his mouth and says nothing. He waves a useless hand, taking in the barn.

Ellie doesn't know what to say next.

They hear a noise, it's her mother, standing in the slab of light, the open doorway.

Barry strides past his daughter. 'I'll be back soon, Ellie, see you then eh?'

Ellie follows him out, watches while he locks the door.

He and Sharon have a brief exchange—a yelling match, and then he's gone. Ellie hears his ute door blam, watches the dust rise after him up the road.

*

Ellie and Sharon fight. They fight a lot these days. Stand facing each other, feet firmly planted, screaming, both of them red in the face. The little ones begin to bawl. The house is filled with misery. Sharon picks up a hairbrush, and advances on the girl. Ellie screams, thumps out the door, across the clearing and into the trees.

She picks her way above the khaki-coloured river, high and fast-flowing after all the rain. In the evening of still light, a soft pink line is drawn above the ridge; lips closing upon the day.

She blunders down a narrow track, prickly shrubs catch at her clothes. I hate her, I hate them all, she mutters aloud, balling up her fists.

She's arrested by a movement on the far bank, a flicker at the corner of her eye. It's a small flock of wild goats, leaping amongst the strewn boulders at the river's edge as they make their way down to the water. Vermin, thinks Ellie. If I had a gun, I'd shoot them. She stands stock still, screened by bushes, watches the mothers' dipping muzzles, the kids playing, rearing together like dogs, wagging tiny tails. The billy goat with his long curved horns stands guard upon a rock, his blunt head turning, looking this way and that, scanning the scrub with his yellow eyes. He's an old goat, thinks Ellie, an old warrior, battered and scarred. She can see the corrugations of his ribs, the rough texture of his scraggy hide. Then it seems he's staring right at her, looking into her, she and the goat frozen like statues. She can see into his soul, his feral, goaty nature. She's not sure how long it lasts—but the moment breaks with a secret signal and the whole flock is on the move, bounding over rocks and into the scrub, disappearing amongst the trees.

Ellie moves along the side of the house in the almost-dark, moons amongst upturned pot-plants of long ago, the mess of river rocks that was to make a garden. Glances in a window as she passes, and there is her mother's face looking out, pink and strained. When she enters the kitchen she sees her mother's still angry with her. But Ellie has forgotten what they were fighting about.

'Where were you?' snaps Sharon, 'I needed a hand.'

'I'm leaving,' Ellie says, 'I'm going to live with Dad.'

Her mother turns back to her baking. Says sadly, 'He doesn't want you, love. He has another family now.'

Ellie runs outside again. A moon like a jerky grin is riding the scrub. It's cold—there's nowhere to go. When she goes back in, the little boys smirk and won't do what she tells them, until she slaps one of them hard on his pink freckled cheek, causing him to howl.

*

The big barn is a galvanised iron shell in a field of lupins. Barry had built it to house all his junk, the stuff he collected over the years, as the house was too small to hold it all, and Sharon wouldn't let him fill it up with rubbish. The fact that the space was there attracted more things, until the barn was full.

When he returned, out of the blue, his idea was to auction off everything in the barn, as well as the old truck, rusting in the paddock, and the railway carriage, that was going to be accommodation for backpackers, but which had stood empty for years.

Sharon decides she might as well make something out of the auction and organises a tea, coffee, cold drinks, cake and sandwiches stall, aided by Ellie and a couple of local teenage girls.

The whole district turns up for the auction. Everyone's dying to know what Barry has kept hidden in that barn all these years. Everyone wants a look. The horse paddock becomes a carpark, filled with enough cars to rival any gymkhana or show-day turn-out. It's a clear, hot day, and the lines of cars are bright beads in the sun. Sharon's boys stampede around, over-excited, frantic for any trouble they might get themselves into.

The hot, dim barn is crowded with people and things. Farmers stand sweaty in their Blundstones as the auctioneer moves from item to item, chanting to the dance of waving hands. A Blackwood china cabinet, an iron bedstead, an urn, a chainsaw, a blockbuster, a plough, toolboxes, a dress-dummy. People stand around guffawing, joking behind their hands over the crates of dusty bottles of milky viscous mutton bird oil, that great cure-all, half buried by rusty dog chains, assorted screws, nails, old Women's Days peppered with rat-shit. God only knows, they say, what scorpions nests lie buried beneath the grot.

Barry sells everything—his one-ton truck, the railway carriage, a couple of buggies, harnesses stiff and white with mould. He sells car wheels, tyres, a trailer, a rusty circular saw, a single-bar radiator, a transistor radio, a pine-wood table he'd made himself. He sells weatherboards, sheets of roofing iron, stained-glass windows he'd taken from derelict farm houses. He sells a box of plates he'd found at the tip.

What remains is bought up by a local secondhand dealer whose shop is filled with similar stuff. Later, it's said under tomcat piss stained rags the man finds a rough wooden box, and inside it a pair of pristine ceramic Chinese pots from the gold-rush days, worth a mint.

Sharon bustles behind trestle tables laid out with sandwiches, scones and cake. Old women perch on numbered auctioned chairs on the side of the hill and munch like cows.

Evening. An old club lounge squats on the hill, the long paddock grass tickling its skirts. A few yards away is a battered rusted canary cage, a flapping number taped to its side. All that's left of a life, muses Barry, hands on hips. Feels the fatness of his wallet. Not bad. He swivels on his heels, hearing giggling behind his back. A boy's orange head bobs back behind the barn. He thinks vaguely, he ought to give them something—even though most of them aren't even his. As the last cars back out of the paddock, he glances at his watch. Beer o'clock. The pub swims into his mind, his local, the ruddy faces that'll greet him there, some friendly, others not, the ones that sided with Sharon.

When he looks up, it's the girl-she's standing by the ute, holding a stuffed-full day-pack by the straps.

Her mouth is firm, reminding him of the mother. 'I'm coming with you.'

'No.' He tries to make it sound gentle. 'You can't Ellie.'

'Why not?'

'I can't look after you.' His throat is dry, he's had a long day. 'You're better off here, with your mother.' He doesn't need this.

He starts to stride toward the ute, but the girl gets hold somehow, of his hand. He leans down to her, grips her thin upper arms. Glances over to the house where her mother is watching, arms folded, standing by the door.

'I'll write to you,' he says. 'Ok?'

'But I want to live with you,' she says, in a whiny voice.

'You can't. The court said you have to live with Sharon. I can't do nothing about it. Now, I have to be off, Ellie, be a good girl, ok?' He fumbles in his pocket, and puts something in her hand—a small hard thing wrapped in an envelope.

Ellie watches the ute drive away, disappearing and reappearing up the humpy road. Jolts up her arm in a wave, and lets it fall. Swallows down the lump which flows into her chest and nestles, a rock. She unwraps the envelope and stares at the key, small and silver in her palm. But drops it, kicks it under the dirt. She doesn't want his old empty barn. 'I'm leaving,' she whispers to herself.

There's a quietude about the land. She looks out across the clearing to the line of bluish bush beyond. Her mother's voice cracks the silence. Ellie begins to trudge back to the house, but turns and heads toward the river. She pauses on the ridge, hopes for a glimpse of the feral flock.

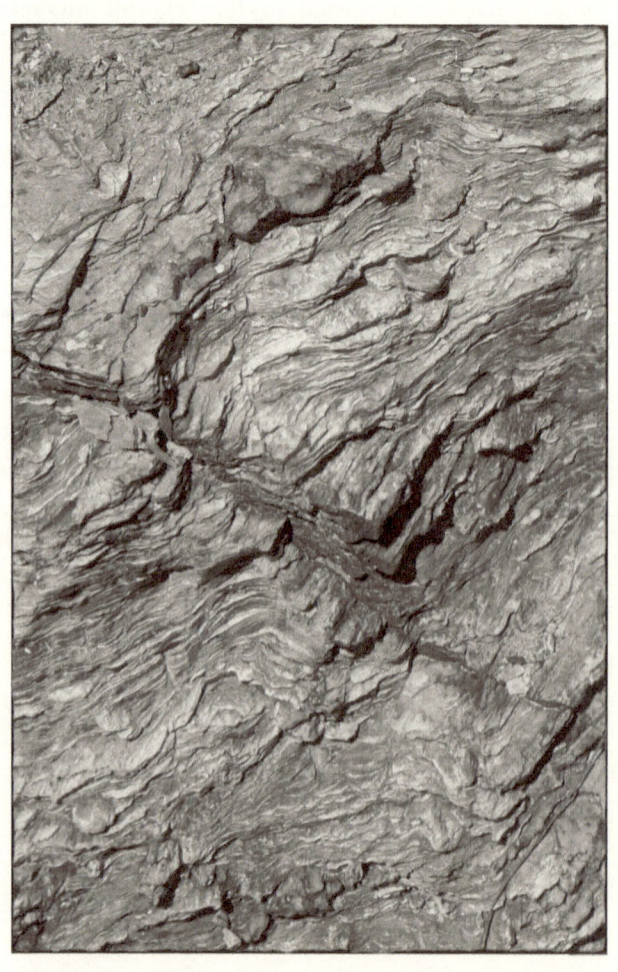

STONES

He was standing on the edge of a great gorge, into which there was no need to throw himself because he had experienced every stone of it already.

Patrick White

As he walked further away from the houses, he felt eyes slide away from him. Hands that would press down on him let go.

He followed the road until it ended in a cul-de-sac, edged by blocks of land not yet built upon, and found a path that led into the bush. It was the place where people dumped rubbish at night. Refuse, toilet paper, wreathed the bushes. An ancient fridge, a plastic bag of disposable nappies and further in, an old car body, a station wagon, now a brittle rust shell.

He found a rock and sat upon it smoking, feeling the cold drive into his bony backside. There was a slight fluttering on his trousers and he looked down to see a leech somersaulting on his leg. He touched it with his fag end and it shrivelled like a spent balloon, causing him to laugh out loud.

The sound of his own laughter was strange to him in the quiet of the bush. He realised the bush was not completely silent—an amplified, staccato voice started up on the ridge where the houses were. The voice stopped, and it was quiet again, until he became aware of the distant highway, and parrots grating in the scrub around him.

He looked about. Deeper in, the bush was unspoilt and not yet infested with weeds. He knew little or nothing of the Australian bush, but saw there was a pattern in the arrangement of foliage, repeated over and over. Twisted trees grew between and even over the surface of the grey sparkling rocks. Scattered throughout were bushes with small spiny red flowers, and others with hairy yellow cones.

He followed the path up a slight incline and glanced back to the bright, startled roofs of the houses. Then they were gone, obliterated by trees. There was a new feeling that struck him in the chest-he was suffocated by the scrub in which he was now immersed.

He found the cave easily. It was on the edge of an escarpment, below the white rock that emerged above the bush, a rock convoluted like a brain. He imagined the cave was the entrance to a honeycomb within. A labyrinth of chambers connected by secret passageways.

His cave was on the edge of a vista almost too dramatic, too terrible to look at. The great bowl of a blue valley was awash with distant creeks, the shadows of slow-moving, magisterial clouds patterned the tops of the trees.

The cave had been made liveable by a German hiding out during the Second World War, and since then had been occupied by homeless man after homeless man. A brick wall, partly demolished, screened the cave's mouth as well as the view, and offered some shelter from icy winds. A cistern, constructed of cemented-together rocks, collected water run-off from above.

Scattered around the cave floor were shards of broken glass, bent rusted nails and rusted tins. The walls were etched with worn graffiti, mostly indecipherable, except for FUCK HELL carved across the roof.

He made his bed in a cavity deep in the cave. Beyond, a low tunnel pressed further in, reminding him of the dream.

Months passed. He saw few people. Sometimes he'd hear them tramping on the brain rock above him, pausing to stare into the fish-shaped pools which were surrounded by the ancient marks of axe or spear.

He felt at peace in the peculiar mist of afternoons. These were the good times. He'd squat upon a high jutting rock, grooved like lizard skin, where the afternoon sun illuminated a million motes sparkling in the blue, powdered air. He'd listen to the lyrebirds, their liquid cries emulating all the birds known to that bush—black cockatoo, whipbird, bower bird, noisy miner, and others he couldn't distinguish. One lyrebird made a repetitive sound like the wheezing of a sick machine refusing to start.

He kept himself still as the lyrebirds came closer, tramping and scratching in the thick mulch of the gullies, and would catch sight of the dark shape of a bird, flitting anxiously, tail aloft, between the angophoras.

The salmon trunks of angophoras were twisted into the tortured shapes of human bodies, of women used by child-birth and life. He could see the stretched-out arms, the puckered, worn breasts along the trunk exposed to the hardship of sun and weather. They reminded him of mothers dancing, their bodies sleek in rain.

Upon the trunk of one large old angophora was a bulbous lump, a burl-a head, a face, gazing into bush and gully, forever staring out—at what, he didn't know.

At times the bush held too many faces, eyes. He would then withdraw to his cave, cover himself in his black blanket where memory bled another landscape into the one that immersed him. European trees, pine forests, orderly and straight, imposed themselves on the twisted scrub. Green fields dotted with large black cows, a lake, a red-roofed barn.

He did not wish to be around people, but sometimes would choose to observe them from a distance while on his walks to the village shops.

He would pause beside the rusted car, think of how it would have been driven down an untenable and rough track, before the housing estate with its curved bitumen roads had been built. He imagined a gang of wild boys emboldened by beer, whooping and yelling, rolling the stolen Holden and abandoning it there.

Thoughts of the car stirred an ache within him, a quiver in his guts—something like excitement, as morsels of memory of his own youth arose. Images, scenes—of being with others, a feeling of camaraderie, of being as one. These were disjointed, sketchy. His memory had been mangled by the treatments he'd had. And always, as he tramped toward the cul-de-sac and the beginnings of the houses, the familiar heaviness would descend and lie upon his shoulders—the pressing hands, the inquisitorial eyes.

He preferred to walk along the street at dusk, the median strips, velvet green under streetlights. He liked the autumn evenings most of all, the first chill touching his cheeks. There was a smell of woodfires and drifts of wavy smoke in the darkening sky. Most of the houses were set back, quiet amid

the twitter of crickets. He could see right into the brightly—
lit rooms, though generally he'd avert his eyes. He walked
with a limp, so anyone could tell his peculiar tread.

Once he stood and watched through a bright window a
man in a white shirt cooking dinner, elbow circling above a
frying pan. Could see the smoke, feel it in his throat, as the
smell of steak suffused the surrounding air.

He limped back from the little village along the road
beside the railway line, carrying his plastic bags. He knew
they would come. He bowed his head, felt a cloud descend,
lie heavy on his shoulders, a grey, jelly-like thing.

*

The first time he sees the dog, he thinks it's an hallucination.
The dog appears on the path in the bush, and both man and
dog are frozen, startled. The dog growls softly. The man turns
and walks the other way. The dog follows him at a distance,
sniffing his tracks.

Later, when the man is eating his dinner, he looks up to
see the dog at the entrance to the cave, watching. It is not a
handsome dog. A cross between a cattle dog and something
smaller, it has short legs and a long body. Its mottled fur is
rubbed bald in places. Its front feet turn outwards, giving it a
comical look. The dog sits, and pants, and continues to stare,
until the man sets down his plate. The dog laps up the canned
Irish stew. The man remembers vaguely a German Shepherd
he once owned, how its depthless, yellow eyes would follow
him as he moved from room to room. He thinks of a small
white cluttered house. He remembers snow.

After that time, the dog's eyes do not leave the man. It follows
him along the road to the village, pausing to sniff and cock its
leg. By this time the man's clothes are a mosaic of blacks and

greys, ragged. His wild hair is knotted into Rasta clumps. He has a ratty beard. His teeth are black.

The man has no mirror, doesn't know what he looks like. Doesn't notice the striations upon his hands that resemble an aerial view of the land, the crenated country, the cross-hatch of gully and ridge. He sits upon the rock and the sun burns his head, which is now bald in the middle.

People come. From the brain-like rock he can see the scrub which adjoins the cul-de-sac, and the path through the bush to the road. On a Saturday, an overweight young couple in pastel clothing tack back and forth through a small section of bush. The young couple do not wander off the block. They do not explore the bush beyond. They do not stroll up the brain rock and look at the view. They sit together on a rock on the block. The young man points and gesticulates at scrub and trees. Then they leave.

Months later the bulldozers come. Soil rocks trees are pushed before them and formed into towering piles. The rubbish trail is obliterated. Bulldozers roar all day, the sound reverberates off the gullies, constant, unstoppable. The land is pared back to pink earth, square and flat, and shortly after rings with hammering, and a fragile-looking pine skeleton emerges above the scrub. The man now takes a more circuitous route from his cave to the road, via a path he makes himself, hiding the path's entrance with low-hanging branches.

In the village the man is known as the crazy hermit at the Rock. Living under the Rock, like some bug or insect. He's harmless, they say. He's dangerous, say others.

He's deranged, a mental patient. Some women are scared to walk in the bush alone with him there. He's wise, others say. He's a mystic. He talks to snakes, he charms them. He's rich, say some—he owns four houses. He's a foreigner, say others. He's from Germany, he's Czech, he's from Poland, from somewhere in Europe. He can't speak English, they say. Others say he speaks English very well. I'm glad he's out there, says one. This is an old man who's seen as a bit of a loner himself, who built the first house out along the ridge. He's the eyes and ears out there, says the old man. Taking care of things. It makes me feel safe. If there was a bush-fire, for instance, the hermit would warn us. Though about the last, he's not so sure.

The people in the houses do not enter the bush. The bush laps at the edges of their lawns, the borders of their properties. The lawns yellow in the summer drought, the grass turns spiky and brittle. In mid-autumn, jonquils emerge, bursting forth into buttery clumps, exuding a scent both exotic and familiar. Some of the garden plants run amok, spill over into the bush beyond, creating a strangling, riotous jungle.

The people in the houses look through their windows at a view. They live on the rim of the bush which is like a great sea, the colour, the sound of the sea—the blue air swirling in a gully they dreamily gaze into.

He knows they will come. On one of his walks he sees a trail of torn grey fur that leads to a necklace of delicate glistening intestines and a torn-off possum's arm, the little pink-gloved hand still curled. At night, cocooned in his blankets, he hears the possums sniggering from the trees around the cave.

The dog sleeps with him, cleaves to his body for warmth. It gives him the courage to move further into the chamber. He touches the walls, finding they are egg-shell white, transparent. Rooms open to other rooms. He discovers rooms he never knew existed. The dog pads behind him, even in his dreams. Doors open before him as he wanders the labyrinth. In a sparsely furnished room he finds a pile of photographs on a table. He flicks through. The photos are of two boys, twins, but he remembers that one of them had died. In the dream he cries in the back of his throat, a whine-like keening.

He wakes to the dog, its puzzled face filling his vision. The dog's teeth are long and white. It is not an old dog—it only has the appearance of being old, like the man. The dog belonged neither to the bush nor the civilised world. Dumped, it had foraged in the strip between the backyards and the bush before attaching itself to the man.

It had been spotted by neighbours, rocks were hurled at it if it approached, and so it had become timid. But the dog was never afraid of the man, perhaps because the man didn't smell of soap, of suburban homes; the man had his own strong smell—smoky, reasty, tangible.

In the mornings, the dog would lick the man awake, his tongue flicking his nostrils, so that the first thing the man saw was the benign face of the dog, its eyes boring into his. The man never tied a lead to the dog—the dog went where the man went, following at heel, its snout nudging the man's calf, or trotting out in front, head down, ears forward, pausing to sniff and cock its leg on clumps of grass.

The dog had a penchant for the canned Irish stew that the man bought at the store in the village. The dog would gobble it as it slid from the can—a whole can-shaped brown jellied lump of it.

When he first got the dog, people began to greet the man and smile at the dog as they passed them along the road. But the man was aloof and so was the dog. The dog would not come toward questing hands or allow himself to be touched.

If other dogs approached he would stand stiff-legged, the hair on his back raised, before daintily circling to sniff.

The man would never call out to the dog—he would limp on ahead, as if the dog wasn't there. He did not act like he was the dog's owner—the dog was an appendage or a shadow, a sometime minder.

The people of the village remarked over the years that the dog and the man were very much alike; they began to look alike—the dog's ash-flecked fur resembling the variegated appearance of the man.

Sometimes the dog would wander off on its own, lunge after a wallaby, or snout its way along the fences of the houses that backed to the bush, drawn by the scent of compost bins and chickens and other dogs. National Parks were rung on a number of occasions, and so was the RSPCA, but the cunning dog disappeared before they got there.

The man would wait until the dog returned before cooking and eating his dinner. He did not have a name for the dog, he didn't speak to the dog, but he would pat its head with the flat of his hand.

On a day of unprecedented wind, the dog is seen amongst the debris of over-turned wheelie-bins, running off with a disposable nappy in his mouth. The RSPCA arrives in a white van and a young man with a noose on a pole, captures the dog at the side of the road as it pauses to eat from its find. The dog whines softly in his throat and twists wildly around as he's levered into the van—but the figure of the man is nowhere.

In the evening the man puts out food for the dog and waits. His fire licks the cave's walls, illuminating the graffiti, the FUCK HELL sign. He grows apprehensive. He is sure they will come. The cave exerts a strange, primal atmosphere, a smell of shit, fear, damp. When he curls up in his blanket at the back of the cave, the cold drives into him and he misses the warm body of the dog. He falls into an uneasy sleep, sees their faces, all of them young, respectable, their faces open, clean, so clean. The sudden crowd of them before his bed, the student doctors, revealed when they drew back the curtain. The lone woman amongst them the only one whose expression changed, who's eyes widened when he screamed, as he tried to rise against the restraints.

He battles all night in hospital wards, under yellowish fluorescent light, his body racked against stony surfaces, fists hitting the dead-end doors at the ends of corridors. He presses his face against the glass, the opaque windows, trying to make out the blurry shifting forms beyond. He wakes at times, and is reassured by the crumbly honey-rock he lies against, the warm ochre of his fire's embers, but always returns to the dream, to their faces, their eyes, their reaching hands.

At dawn he's exhausted. He's a bundle of rags he's a pile of sticks. He drags himself into the open, above the valley's cauldron of cloud.

He stands shakily in weak morning sun, leans into the cistern to drink. A dark shape spreads across the water.

He looks up—hanging in the sky's lair is a huge cloud, a nimbus, anvil-shaped, a fretwork of silver round its edges. It hovers above him, and advances, arms outstretched, ready to enclose.

He scrambles blind through whipping scrub. The stones spring up and roll tumble with him as he half-runs, falls careening amongst the trees, no longer feeling pain. He crashes through splintered blue.

The cliff's bland, flat faces gaze past him. The head in the tree, forever looking away. Silence except for the lyrebirds' entwined cries, their imitation whips cracking the sharp air.

*

A stranger arrives in the village, a foreigner. He carries a day-pack stuffed with flyers, tacks them up on lampposts and message boards in shops. Have you seen him? he asks people, pointing to the image of the missing man, a young man, nice-looking. It could've been him when he was younger, the bloke at the Rock, the locals tell him, but it's hard to say. They direct the stranger to the cave.

The stranger stands at the cave entrance and peers inside. The cave looks abandoned, although some signs of habitation remain: a bundle of black blankets in a corner, a few dented, disarrayed cooking pots and rusted tins. Not here, he thinks, was he ever? The cave smells like a urinal. The stranger imagines what might go on in the cave at night.

The stranger turns from the cave and scans the dizzying valley: cloud shadows edge across the tree canopy—one like a flattened cat which turns into a curled-up woman. The wind in the scrub of the escarpment sounds like surf brewing on a beach. The air is misty with spray from blown-back waterfalls.

The man feels hollowed-out, his loneliness magnified by the immensity of the landscape, the weighty cumulations of cloud. The wind almost shuts his eyes, it could blow him away.

He steadies himself, holding onto the brick wall at the cave entrance. He takes a flyer from his day-pack and stares at the image of his brother for some time. Then he secures it under a rock on the wall, and leaves.

The wind dislodges the flyer, flicks it into the scrub of the escarpment, where it catches against the shrubs with spiky flowers. The flyer travels through the valley on the wind, a small, white curl of paper. The young man in the picture is looking into the distance, past the photographer, whose shadow is still visible in the foreground. He does not look at the photographer or the viewer, he sees further, beyond anything human.

LOOKING AFTER CECILY

We've been on the road for days and now I'm back, under the massive Moreton Bay figs, the white sky rushing behind sheltering leaves. I'm digging at the soles of my shoes with a stick, picking out smashed fruit and leaf-litter, just like the old days. It's a kind of Eden. I remember when I first came out here—Adam, the first boy.

It's different now, more like a park than a bin, with people throwing sticks for dogs and picnickers settling down within sight of the wards. I can smell the nearby river, where rowers skim in uniform strokes. The grounds are unkempt. Everything's taller and more over-grown. They must've finally got rid of him, old Gurgller. The wards have shrunk to a few buildings, and the mad sit outside in faded pyjamas, playing chess at plastic tables. A woman in a nightie strikes off into the plantains, now and then letting out a peacock screech.

The creek is still here, though its drier now, only a trickle, and tadpoles wriggle in the ponds where huge goldfish once poked their snouts at the surface and gobbled at a shower of crumbs. Elephant ears stampede along the creek's edge, amongst a riot of ornamental ginger and out-of-control day lilies. Gurgller—if you are dead—your ghost must be snapping ineffectual pruning shears.

My favourite park-bench is still here—scabby and rotting under the stand of bamboo—and I sit and rest, my long legs splayed, the bamboo knocking like Japanese music. I unwrap the chocolate bar that is almost welded to my shirt pocket, and bite into it.

I'm hungry, tired and in need of peace, after being in the car with that lot. Three days straight, driving. The car—the Falcon—is up on the street, illegally parked, hot and ticking, headlights plastered with smashed grasshoppers. Long brown feathers stick out of the radiator vents, from when Cecily couldn't stop in time for the coucal that dashed across the road in front of her. Coucals are silly birds. They wait at the roadside and run out when they see you coming. Still, I don't like to see them hit—it could bring bad luck.

When Cecily hit the bird we all shrieked at her. She slammed on the brakes, got out and went round and stared at the front of the car. She told us it was nothing, but we knew. Cecily ought to know—she should not, must not, lie to us.

There were always too many lies. When I first came out it was here, the day after they left—those people who were the parents. Boys are tough and independent, and don't cry. Boys get on with things, so when Cecily found out they weren't coming back, I took over for a while.

Oh yes, there were parents, brothers and sisters. A whole family. Father could not put up with a child with problems. Mother wept and protested, but she was under his thumb. In those days, things like that could happen to children. You could get dumped in a looney-bin just because they thought you had epilepsy.

They wouldn't do that to a child these days—or would they? Cecily thought our parents went to the United States. That's why they didn't visit. They had to leave, she said, the police were after them, because my father had stolen some money from the bank where he worked, and if he were caught the whole family would be broken up. That's what Cecily told people.

Boys are useful when there are things to do, like carry the wood, or wash the car, or fix things. I'm itching right now to go up to the car and open the hood and check everything, scrape the insects off the windscreen, even though I'm exhausted.

Cecily wondered how things like that got done. The doctors told her, but she never truly believed until the day before we left, when Dr Steve showed her the video. The video of Cecily changing. Taken a year ago at his clinic. Dr Steve had decided that Cecily was ready. She watched and saw all of us. She saw me, Adam, the first boy. She saw little Sarah, and baby Amber, who holds all the memories. She saw Cristobel, who she didn't like. She saw Mikey, who had come out when Gurgller did things to Cecily in the garden shed. She even saw The Interrogator, and Old Needlehead.

She moved up close to the big tv and saw her expressions change. How even her features seemed to alter with each new part. How when the little ones came out, her skin softened, her eyes widened, her brow uncreased.

She watched as little Sarah took out the teeth and threw off the shoes, as she always does.

Cecily stared. She grew pale and trembly. Doctor Steve, young and kind, knelt down beside her. He took her hand.

Now Cecily, he said, you can see why your teeth disappear from out of your head and why you can never find your shoes anywhere. It explains the lost time, the voices. It doesn't mean you are mad, he said.

Cecily looked up at Dr Steve. He was her favourite. She trusted him. I also like Dr Steve, he has such kind, brown eyes. I don't like to listen when some of the others say that Dr Steve is only looking out for his own career.

Dr Steve squeezed Cecily's hand. Think of yourself as a main character in a story. When you were young, when something bad happened, you made up new characters to help out. Those characters are still with you. But it's your story, Cecily.

So many, so many, Cecily moaned. That's all she would say, all the way home. We weren't sure what she meant. So many parts, or so many bad things? And as she drove home Old Needlehead whispered in her ear, Dr Steve said it was a story-he thinks you're making it up.

When she got home she went straight to the bathroom cabinet. She lined up the pill bottles and each of us took a handful. She lay down on the bed. But then Gina, who was a nurse for twenty years, and highly responsible, came out and called an ambulance.

At the hospital they made us drink charcoal. We didn't like it. They lied to us and treated us like we were bad. They talked about us in front of us as though we were deaf. So I got us up, and pulled out the drip, and got us home to pick up the car.

Cecily didn't know what was going on. One minute she was taking pills, the next minute she was in a car, driving, heading south. It's a battered old car, but a good one. It was hot and close in there, though, with all of us. It was my idea.

I thought it might cheer her up. She likes a journey, does Cecily. Travelling takes you out of yourself, she says. It's like dying. A different kind of consciousness, separate from everyday things. There is comfort and safety in flight, she's told us. You can go and go and never arrive.

The little ones soon got bored, that was the problem. At one point three of them were crying at once and Cecily was going mad from all the screaming. We pulled up at a roadhouse, a big one, with road trains parked in the driveway. I wanted to hang around and inspect them, to marvel at the size of the tyres. Mikey, always one for the great outdoors, wanted to go off hiking in the scrub and check out the tall termite mounds he'd seen from the road. Amber saw the cockatoo in its cage by the door and began to cry because it had a disease that was making it bald. Then Cristobel decided to have a tantrum because she wanted fruit-loops.

Cecily ended up stuck in the middle of the driveway, hands clamped to her ears and stamping her feet. Cecily, I hissed at her. Get it together, people are staring.

With that she got herself into the loo and locked the door. She stared at herself in the smeared mirror, breathing hard. Then she addressed all of us. I'm fifty-eight years old, she gasped. I've had just about enough of you kids. We will eat first, she said, and then we will play pinball. Then we will look at the trucks and then, the termite mounds. After that I am going to take some photos. She composed herself, powdered her nose and walked outside. Us kids shut up and let it all unfold. She let Mikey order sausages and chips, and Cristobel had fruit-loops and milk for dessert. Cecily smoked a cigarette while I looked at the trucks, and no-one said anything about how smoking is bad for our health.

Back in the car, I thought, man, she's listening to us at last. She's working with us, like Dr Steve said she should. She's managing us. We are co-operating. When we drove off I felt like we were getting it together. I felt a sense of freedom, hope for the future. We sang as we drove, all the old pop songs we knew and ads and tv shows. *Rollin, rollin rollin*, we sang, *RAWHIDE*. We stopped for breaks behind the bushes, squatting on the hard, quartzy ground, where your piss does not sink in and splashes your leg.

But after Cecily hit the coucal, she grew despondent. She was tired. She wasn't concentrating on the road, and sometimes she'd swerve and skid in the gravel. I was afraid we'd hit something worse than a coucal, a cow or a tree, so I took over.

I'm only ten, but I can drive all right. Down the long straight roads of Western NSW. Through bull-dust scrub, past dozing cattle that struggled up at the sight of us.

We needed a destination; we couldn't drive forever. That's when I thought of bringing us down here, all the way to Sydney. Back to my first home, where I first began. We needed a sanctuary, an asylum. That's what this place is. A kind of Eden. It was designed that way. Even though it's gone to seed in some wild-blown way.

I drove us over the Harbour Bridge and all the little ones jumped up and down on the seats. Waved at the Opera House that sat like a big white shining insect on the rim of the harbour. The little ones distracted me so much I couldn't figure out what lane to be in and ended up screaming at them as we drove into an endless wilderness of city streets and stop-start traffic. It was exciting for all of us—the kids smeared up the windows, goggling, craning up at the blue-glass towers.

Cecily woke up driving along Parramatta Road and couldn't for the life of her figure out how she got there. What have you done? Where are we going? was all she could say, over and over. When we told her, she panicked. Oh no, I can't go there, she shrieked, not after what they did to me..

Then Old Needlehead tuned in and said, eh Cecily, you could head to that rowing club beside the hospital, drive down the ramp and right into the river. That'd fix it all, wouldn't it—all the suffering.

Cecily had been tempted by the idea of drowning herself in the river when we lived at the hospital all those years. Here's your chance, cried Old Needlehead. What've you got to live for anyway. More of the same?

But then I came out and Cecily couldn't do it. I've told Needlehead over and over, if you kill the host you kill yourself and you kill all of us, don't you get it? I've often wondered what would happen to us if she did kill herself. Whether there's only one soul—Cecily's, or if we have one each. If Cecily dies would five or eight or more of us float out of her still body, or would we become whole at that instant—integrated, as the doctors say when they talk text-book. It makes me wonder, what are people anyway?

I'm exhausted, I've really had it. Sitting on my favourite old bench under the bamboo is relaxing, but me and Gina can't stay out forever. We get tired, and when we sleep, who knows what could happen. Us good ones could organise ourselves into shifts, but the trouble is, you can't trust the littlies. Old Needlehead could trick them, or they could doze off and Cecily might wake up again, and take herself down to the water. Old Needlehead put the idea into her head and she's taken with it. She'll kill us all.

Me and Gina have a plan. In a minute I'll gather myself up, and head right over to the ward. I'll saunter up the concrete paths between the ponds, through all the rioting foliage. I'll cross the shaved lawn, and the patients sitting out the front will turn and stare in my direction. Wait'll you see this, I'll think, wait'll you see. I'll walk right up the steps and into the dim and cool hall, where a lazy fan stirs all the smells—disinfectant, mince and medication. I'll stand against the yellowish wall, and call out someone who's out of control, like Cristobel, who'll have a tantrum, and then one of the bad ones, like the Interrogator.

I'm sick and tired of looking after Cecily, I hope someone else will take charge for a change. I'll put on my best show yet, a change every five seconds. That'll make the nurses come running.

ACKNOWLEDGEMENTS

I would like to thank editor Linda Godfrey for her discernment and keen eye, and publisher Bronwyn Mehan for providing the opportunity to bring these stories together as a collection. Warm thanks to Associate Professor Anna Gibbs of the Writing and Society Research Group, University of Western Sydney, for her encouragement over the years. To Dr Virginia Shepherd, who read and critically commented on drafts of these stories, and was always insightful. My thanks to Varuna Writers Centre, particularly to Helen Barnes-Bulley and Carol Major. And to my writing friends for their affirmation of my work. (You know who you are.)

Grateful acknowledgement is made to the following publications in which earlier versions of the stories appeared. 'The lives of the dead' short story was first published in Overland's online journal *Overland Express*. 'Before the wave' appeared in *Overland Magazine*, and 'Menace' in *Going Down Swinging*. 'Earth eaters', 'the cradle arms of strangers' and 'looking after Cecily' were published in *Hecate: A Women's Interdisciplinary Journal*. 'The fool' was included in *Australian Short Stories,* and 'at the fence' in *Island Magazine*. 'Stones' appears in the anthology *Things that are found in trees and other stories* (Margaret River Press).

The line quoted on p.115 is from the short story, 'A Woman's Hand' by Patrick White, in *The Cockatoos: Shorter Novels and Stories*, (Jonathan Cape, London, 1974) p.91. Reprinted with the permission of Barbara Mobbs, on behalf of Patrick White.

ALSO BY SPINELESS WONDERS

A treasure trove of writing from some of the most innovative practitioners of prose poetry and microfiction in Australia. KABITA DHARA, EDITOR, READINGS MONTHLY

Small Wonder
prose poems & microfiction

edited by Linda Godfrey and Julie Chevalier

Here are short and clever pieces by thirty contemporary Australian writers on the eroticism of mashed potato, parenting as magic realism and a tongue-in-cheek history of the Cyclops bicycle. Includes award-winning writers Michael Farrell, Keri Glastonbury, Judith Beveridge and Peter Boyle. Features prose poems and microfiction selected by competition judge joanne burns.
Contains illustrations by talented young artist, Paden Hunter.

Quality short Australian fiction, packed with surprises.
Prepare to be transported. MARION HALLIGAN

Escape
anthology of short stories

edited by Bronwyn Mehan

ESCAPE has unexpected tales of contemporary life,
comedy, tragedy, mystery, romance, sci-fi, dystopian
fantasy, a homage to David Foster Wallace and lots
more. .
Features award-winning writers such as Ryan O'Neill,
Jen Mills, Andy Kissane, Louise Swinn, Julie Chevalier,
A.S. Patrić and Kim Westwood, as well as stories chosen
by Sophie Cunningham in the inaugural Carmel Bird
Short Fiction Award.

Unflinching realism ... compelling and complex in equal measure. THE AUSTRALIAN

Permission to Lie

by Julie Chevalier

In this wonderfully diverse collection, Chevalier does not flinch from delving into some of the messier aspects of contemporary Australian culture, whether inside prisons, nudist camps or in cut-throat boardrooms. Cover art and six pages of quirky illustrations by Paden Hunter.

'A new voice in Australian fiction, wry, gritty, knowing and true.' **Fiona McGregor**

Indelible Ink

The Rattler
& other stories

by A.S. Patrić

This entertaining collection is set in and around contemporary Melbourne. Sometimes serious, sometimes seriously playful—always written in breathtakingly beautiful prose.

Cover art and illustrations by Miles Allinson.

Newton-John, who wields a superb descriptive talent.

Fault Lines

by Pierz Newton-John

Seamless prose, undercurrents of contemporary music, the urbane writing, the suburban settings, but it is all happening behind closed doors.

'Here are the fault lines in all our lives, and Newton-John, with an unflinching eye and a mesmerising style, lays them bare in this sequence of expertly crafted vignettes. Fault Lines returns the grit to the Australian literary landscape.'

Matthew Condon
Trout Opera

'Manning's odd, off-kilter world is strangely addictive .'
JENNIFER MILLS, OVERLAND

Damaged In Transit

by Mary Manning

A person fitting on a suburban train challenges the equilibrium of urbane commuters and the weird guy jotting down words in the mall is about to commit an unspeakable crime. In Manning's fractured future worlds, sexual partners are purchased and returned like commodities and language, culture and religion are all dealt a body blow.

Manning has an original, confident style and a sharp eye for the weaknesses and idiosyncracies of human nature.   **Kerryn Goldsworthy**
Sydney Morning Herald

Stoned Crows
& other Australian icons

edited by Linda Godfrey and Julie Chevalier

What do our best wordsmiths have to say about
Australian icons? This anthology takes a fresh look at
everything from the HIH collapse to crocs, Margaret
Olley, bush burials and the ABC. We visit a post-
apocalyptic Opera House and spend Saturday night in
downtown Byron Bay. Tones range from nostalgic to
sceptical, from wry to LOL.

EARWORMS

short Australian audio

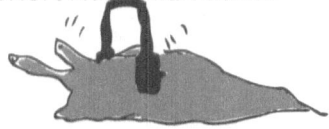

Stories that stay with you

Earworms are those songs with unforgettable hooks that get stuck in your head but Spineless Wonders brings you short Australian earworms—stories by award-winning writers that you definitely won't want to forget.

Stuck in a queue? Don't stress. You can listen to our selection of funny, political and thought-provoking prose poems and microfiction from our anthology, *Small Wonder*.

Got a pile of washing-up or ironing to do? Housework's not a chore when you can listen to short fiction from our anthology, *Escape*.

Commuting every day? Traffic jams are not a problem when you can listen to the latest in contemporary short fiction from Spineless Wonders.

Prices range from $0.99 to $2.99. Gift vouchers available.

Listen to our audio trailers now at
www.shortaustralianstories.com.au.

www.ingramcontent.com/pod-product-compliance
Lightning Source LLC
Chambersburg PA
CBHW050406110726
47899CB00008B/2673